"What would y[ou]
of our marriage, Ellis?"

Ellis pondered Gideon's mocking question.

"A home where I want to live," she said steadily. "Also, a father for Davey."

"You forget something, Ellis." Gideon's eyes burned with a cold flame. "You're offering to buy me, and I believe in giving full value for money!"

"You can always refuse," she countered, feeling threatened. "If you can't stand the heat, get out of the kitchen."

"Oh, I can stand the heat, Ellis. The question is, can you?" His fingers lifted her chin as his eyes roved over her face insolently. "Not bad," he said softly. "Good bone. But a bit of a wild look in the eye...."

Gideon was acting as if he were buying *her*. Why, wondered Ellis, did it hurt so much?

Jeneth Murrey was involved in a near-fatal road accident some years ago that changed her life. During her long convalescence she read romance novels from her local library until she'd read them all. She then sat down and wrote one of her own and went on to make writing her career. She and her husband live in a small North Wales village and enjoy ''gypsying'' around the continent in their camper during holidays.

Books by Jeneth Murrey

HARLEQUIN ROMANCE

HARLEQUIN PRESENTS

Impulsive
Proposal

Jeneth Murrey

Harlequin Books

TORONTO • NEW YORK • LONDON
AMSTERDAM • PARIS • SYDNEY • HAMBURG
STOCKHOLM • ATHENS • TOKYO • MILAN

Original hardcover edition published in 1989
by Mills & Boon Limited

ISBN 0-373-03039-8

Harlequin Romance first edition March 1990

CHAPTER ONE

'. . . AND for the third time, Martin, the answer is "No". I'm very fond of you, you've been a good friend since Robert died, so let's keep it that way.'

Ellis Blake tried hard to look firm and sound decisive but her appearance was against her. Small and slender, pale and nearly platinum-blonde, she had an air of fragility which was deceptive. Her late husband had always likened her to tempered steel, shatterproof. Whereas her would-be suitor—who didn't know her so well—merely grinned and took her at face value.

'Think about it again, Ellis,' he advised, not a bit disturbed by her refusal. 'You need somebody . . .'

'I already have somebody!' She chuckled softly and her silvery eyes twinkled between fringes of long, dark lashes, while her softly passionate mouth curved into a wide, gamine grin. 'Davey's only five years old but he's very careful of me.'

'He's growing up.' Martin's expression was ingenuous, like a wheedling schoolboy's. 'Soon, he'll need a stronger hand than yours. I could look after you both, and it would have its advantages, you know. Moneywise, I'm a whiz. I'm also house-trained, eat anything and I've no bad habits. Besides, it's nearly three years since Robert died and he asked me to take care of you if ever anything happened to

5

him.'

'But I don't love you, Martin.' She had said it before—twice—and she said it again while her ears were stretched to catch any unusual noise from upstairs. 'Oh, dear,' she attempted to laugh it off. 'You choose the most awkward times to propose. I've just sent Davey to bed; heaven knows what he'll be up to while my back's turned.'

'That's what I mean.' Martin was persistent. 'You need a baby-sitter, and I'm a man of many talents. Damn it, I know you don't love me yet, but you could learn to.'

Ellis sighed; it would be so easy to say 'yes' and it would save so much hassle, but it wouldn't be right. She looked at him gravely, as if she were seeing him for the first time. He was quite attractive, in a blunt, unfinished way; he was also intelligent, good-humoured and a marvellous accountant. He'd make any woman a good husband—but not her!

'You already take most of the burden off my shoulders,' she pointed out. 'I don't know what I'd do without you, especially when the tax man cometh.'

'The point is, I love you.'

'No you don't.' She essayed another small chuckle and tried the effect of a bit of weak humour. 'You're only after Robert's money!'

The weak humour went down very well. Martin grinned engagingly, not a bit upset; he knew she didn't mean it. 'And as I said, *I* don't love *you*,' she concluded with as much finality as she could muster.

'You didn't love Robert when you married him,' he reminded her. 'Don't forget, I was there. I knew all about it. You and Robert marrying so he could adopt the baby; I *had* to know, didn't I? Tax and all the other things. If you'd been the boy's mother it would have made everything much easier.'

'Sorry!' she murmured, and teased a reluctant twinkle into his eyes.

'And so you should be.' His grin widened. 'Robert had me and his solicitor; plus a Queen's Counsel feller working on it round the clock to make that adoption watertight. I swear I didn't sleep for a week, what with setting up that trust fund for Davey and all the rest of the hoo-hah. Robert was a firm believer in having everything done *now*! He said you could vouch for Davey's parents . . .'

'Mmm.' She nodded regretfully. 'When Robert and I were married, a great many of his friends thought I'd been his mistress as well as his secretary and that Davey was our child. That used to please him; he was very touchy on the subject and he encouraged them to go on thinking it. At first I was so embarrassed I nearly died of shame, but after a while I learned to ignore it. But you'd met his real mother—my foster sister—so you knew better.'

'Oh, I did!' Martin grinned. 'But I'd have had less work if the gossip had been true,' he mourned. 'Especially when Davey's mother scarpered and left you holding the baby, although even that had its advantages; the scarpering, I mean. That red-headed witch from Wales made big green eyes at Robert—he was always easy game for a sob-story—I didn't feel safe about him until he married you. However, he paid my bill, a thumping big one, without turning a hair.'

'I wasn't good enough for Robert, I didn't love him, not then,' she wanted to say and the silver of her eyes darkened to pewter-grey with the shadows of memory. 'But I learned to love him,' she whispered almost inaudibly, and a fond smile curved her mouth. 'Robert was a very lovable man.'

'So am I.' His face creased into a smile. 'So why can't you . . .?'

'No!' Ellis shook her head with certainty. 'I'm not the woman for you, Martin; yours will be along soon—and don't laugh; I'm another Welsh witch from Wales and, although my eyes aren't green, I see these things. She'll be tall, dark and very loving, so don't you dare settle for anything less.'

'You've seen my new secretary!' he accused.

'You mean you've met her already?' Ellis's eyes became gleeful. She had only described the sort of person she thought would suit him best. 'There, I told you! Hang on to her, Martin, and don't propose to me again, please. In a moment of weakness, I might accept for all the wrong reasons and we'd live a cat-and-dog life. We wouldn't suit at all.' Deliberately, she changed the subject. 'I'm taking Davey to Wales, Martin. We're leaving tomorrow morning, it's all arranged.'

'Just the thing.' He reached across the distance separating them and patted her hand clumsily. 'It's been a long winter; you need a holiday.'

Ellis shook her head. 'Not a holiday exactly. I'm going to the funeral of a very dear friend, and we might stay on with my foster mother for a while.'

'Exactly what you should do,' he consoled her without asking any questions, and there were so many he could have asked. Ellis was struck again by his sheer niceness, and it reinforced her determination. She valued Martin's friendship; it was pleasant, easy and—except for when he was proposing—undemanding. She wanted to keep it that way.

'A change of scene; you'll come back fighting fit,' he continued, managing to take all the strain out of the situation by becoming businesslike. 'You have enough money in your current account? Remember, you need mine and old Wimpole's signature for anything over five thousand. But don't stay away too long, Ellis; I shall miss you.' His goodbye kiss was clumsy—it landed on her eyebrow—but a comforting gesture and a few minutes later, he let himself out of the house and she heard the door close quietly behind him.

For a little while, she sat in the dim, unlit room. Old memories were stirring but she refused to dwell on them, and the future was a chancy thing. Perhaps it would be better not to dwell on that either.

Arriving at that decision, she went upstairs to discover how much damage five-year-old Davey had done to the bathroom. A very wet floor and a strong smell of lavender-scented bath crystals greeted her—Davey preferred to smell beautiful—and he had dropped a hand towel in the bath. Nothing dire, so she went along to his bedroom where, as usual, he was wide awake and clamouring for information.

'There's mountains in Wales and I've never seen a mountain.' His dark eyes were saucerlike with anticipation and his newly washed hair was a riot of toffee-coloured curls. 'Teacher says London has everything, but it hasn't got a mountain. Are they like the mountains on the moon?'

'N-no.' Ellis hesitated as old memories came slipping into her mind, resurrecting the part of her which had once been a charity child from South Wales called Ellis Morgan, who had been given a home among the mountains of Middle Wales. Cader Idris, white and beautiful in winter or the bald heights rounded and golden grey in the summer sunlight. Plynlimmon . . . She swept her mind clean ruthlessly.

Forget all the associations that went with the mountains, with everything from the past! 'Hiraeth', homesickness, was a waste of time. It did no good to dwell on memories, they should be swept up and burned; a lesson she had learned but from which she had never profited.

'They're not so tall and not so spiky,' she explained, 'but it's only April so they may still have a bit of snow left on them. You'd like to see that, wouldn't you?' And at his emphatic nod, she dropped a light kiss on his forehead. 'Now, go to sleep, darling, you're going to need it. We've a long journey tomorrow.'

Davey closed his dark eyes obediently, only to flick them open again. 'I can't sleep,' he protested. 'I'm too 'cited. My eyes won't stay shut. Tell me a story, Ellis. Just a little one, please.'

'Time'll go more quickly if I don't.' She smoothed his hair with a loving hand. 'Go to sleep, my little hawk; dream of flying.' Her voice slipped from a laboriously acquired, clipped English pronunciation into a Celtic lilt which almost sang the words and she became, once again, that Ellis Morgan who had put aside dreams for a painful reality.

Once, she had loved a man with all the fierce pain of youth; a man who hadn't loved her. She could still feel the ache of that love, the empty, hurting place in her heart which no other man could ever fill, but emptiness was part of her now and she could ignore it. Cry for the moon, she would not! Not when she had so much else to be grateful for. Which brought her back to Davey and she cuddled him closer.

'Dream you're soaring over the mountains. No,' her arm tightened about him as he made strenuous flapping movements, 'you're a hawk, Davey, not a sparrow; you don't have to flap your wings all the time. They're big and round and you glide on them; and hawks never move their heads when they're hunting. They keep them very still so that their bright, sharp eyes can see the smallest mouse running through the bracken. Sleep, Davey . . .'

'I can't,' he protested on a wide yawn and then, with the ease of childhood, his eyes closed and she felt his body relax. For a few moments, she didn't stir, not until she was sure he wouldn't wake. Meanwhile, she studied his small face closely. At last, she stood up, reassured. The hair colour was wrong, not a bit like his real mother's or his natural father's, and the features were blurred with the plumpness of childhood. Maybe there *was* something about the eyes; the darkness, the occasional clear, direct look, bright and searching like a hawk; but it was so fleeting, it couldn't be pinned down.

The cleaning of the bathroom didn't take long but

there was still a lot more to do and it was better to occupy herself with something physical. Otherwise her mind tended to dwell on the future, which gave her a sick feeling in her stomach. She had nearly reached the point of no return: the arrangements were already made, and she had told Vanno, her foster mother, that, all being well, she was coming. A telephone call perhaps, to say Davey had a bit of a chill? She snorted disdainfully. Excuses solved nothing! Fear had to be conquered.

Composedly, she left the bathroom, closing the door softly and going down the stairs into the dimly lit lounge. She looked at the drinks tray and shook her head firmly. Once, and only once; the night Robert had died, she had tried that way so she knew it didn't work. For her, alcohol wasn't the answer, so with a straight back and her head held high, she swung on her heel and went to the kitchen to make a pot of tea. But her hands were still cold and shaking with nervousness. She spilled water from the kettle on to the immaculate counter and mopped it up ruefully.

There was a vast difference between planning something and carrying it out, and she was letting her nervousness get the better of her. 'Stupid!' she scolded herself aloud, catching sight of her reflection in the mirror on the windowsill and hastily smoothing out the wreck Davey had made of her usually neat hairdo. When she had reduced it to near tidiness and tucked the silvery ends into a hasty French pleat at the back of her head, she surveyed her face and made a droll moue at her reflection.

'What are you looking agonised about?' she

demanded of it, and went on talking aloud to herself. 'This is your opportunity. You've almost made up your mind and you've made your plans, so what are you dithering about now, when it's nearly too late to dither? You can't disappoint Davey, not at this stage. The truth is, you're a coward!'

She pulled a face at her mirrored reflection, which grimaced back at her. Straightening her features, she studied them, and what she saw didn't reassure her. Somehow they lacked the spirited determination she so wanted to see. They looked too soft and wavery for a twenty-six-year-old woman with a mission in life. She tried another expression, raising her chin haughtily and looking down her nose; it made her look cross-eyed and she forced herself to relax and settled her face into the placid nothingness of a china-faced doll. That placidity coupled with her false air of fragility was a good mask to hide behind!

Everything about her seemed to be waiting—was it for what she knew would be coming tomorrow?—and she could feel tension building up. Something was going to happen but the footsteps she could hear in her mind were much closer than tomorrow and she realised she had been expecting that something, expecting it all day. Hadn't that long-ago Ellis Morgan always known when trouble was coming? So, when the doorbell rang an hour later, she felt no surprise, only a sense of fatality and a grim determination not to be swayed as she went quietly along to the hall to open the door.

The man standing there didn't surprise her either. How could he? She had known it would be him. She had always known when he was near!

'Good evening, Gideon.' She made a pretence of self-possession; the perfect hostess even with her hair looking like an ill-made bird's nest. 'What a lovely surprise. *Do* come in.' And her faint smile could easily have been mistaken for one of welcome, but she stood well back so that there was no chance of their touching as he passed her.

'I wasn't expecting you,' she continued. It was a lie, but she congratulated herself on the ease with which she had said it, and now the blow had fallen, she was no longer uncertain. She was Ellis Blake again, a very wealthy, independent widow, and she could be bright, cheerful and brave. 'I was just going to make some tea, or there's coffee if you'd prefer. Shall I take your coat?'

She didn't wait for a reply; she didn't expect one. This man had never accepted anything from her, never indulged in small talk, not with her. He had always either come straight to the point or remained silent. Out of the corner of her eye, she watched him shrug off his sheepskin jacket, darkened across the shoulders with the rain which had also dampened his black hair into crisp curls. He ignored her offer and allowed the jacket to slip down on to the tiled floor of the entrance hall. Proud as ever, she scolded silently. He wouldn't even use her coat-stand! Afraid of catching something?

Leaving the damp coat lying, she led the way through to the lounge while preserving her outward calm. She wasn't dealing with good old, easy-going Martin now. She would have to be extra careful of what she said!

'You walked here in the rain?' She raised a politely

surprised eyebrow and spoke with gentle irony. 'Oh, surely not *all* the way!'

'No, not all the way.' His face was as implacable as stone and there was a corresponding grittiness in his voice but it smoothed out into a lazy, lilting drawl as he eyed her malevolently, with little flames of anger leaping behind the darkness of his eyes. 'Only from the hotel where I'm staying the night. I was told I might have difficulty parking the old Land Rover among all the Porsches and Ferraris in this affluent neighbourhood.'

'My, my.' Her smile was so stiff she could almost feel her face cracking, but Gideon being sarcastic meant he wasn't quite as sure of himself as he usually was. That ought to shorten the odds, and she badly needed to be in there fighting, with something going for her.

'Are you blaming me for living in this part of town?' she continued gently. 'How that reminds me of old times. You remember, Gideon?' She made it sweetly bitter. 'The times when I could never do anything right? They were so frequent,' she mourned. 'At least twelve hours out of every twenty-four!'

'Those times are still with us.' He followed her into the lounge, striding past her across the room to stand and warm his hands before the open fire which she preferred to the drying warmth of central heating. For a Welshman, he was big, overpoweringly so; he seemed to dominate the room, take all the air from it so that she had difficulty finding enough to breathe. 'And you still can't get it right!' He straightened and stood scowling down at her. It was a magnificent scowl, intimidating, but she had seen it before, too many times, so she could ignore it and pretend a great concentration on what he was saying. 'What the hell do you mean by saying you're coming up to my grandfather's funeral. I would have thought you'd have learned a little delicacy . . .'

'Oh! So it's my lack of delicacy which has brought you all the way from Wales,' she sparkled back at him with a very good attempt at insouciance. 'And you with a funeral on your hands! Oh, Gideon!' She widened her grey eyes till they looked big and round. 'I can only take that as a compliment.'

At this point, she lost a bit of control and the insouciance dissolved into sheer bloody-mindedness, while her eyes sparkled like polished steel and the rather sensual curve of her bottom lip hardened into decision. 'Whatever will Plas Dyffryn do for forty-eight hours without your guiding hand at the helm? But just give me one good reason why I shouldn't attend *Taid's* funeral?' She snapped it out belligerently although common sense told her to play it quietly. Common sense! Gideon; her first love, her only real love, had always driven that clean out of her mind. He always could, he always would! The cold emptiness inside her started to ache intolerably.

'That's something *my* delicacy would normally forbid.' He almost snarled the words. 'But if you want it straight, you can have it. You aren't welcome.' He wasn't shouting, but then Gideon never did. He could be foul and evil-tempered in the most dulcet tones. 'And don't call him "*Taid*", he wasn't *your* grandfather . . .'

'I will if I want to,' she cut in childishly. 'It's what

he asked me to call him and I don't see . . .'

'Also,' he ground it out as though she hadn't interrupted, 'you said you would be bringing your little . . .'

'. . . son?' She reinforced her backbone with a thread of steely determination and held her head very erect. 'My late husband adopted him so there's no need to be so old-fashioned. Lots of women have children who are older than their marriages, and if my husband didn't object, why should you? But I think I understand; it's your famous delicacy again, you don't want to upset my feelings.' She took full advantage of his slight hesitation. 'You can say what you think, Gideon. You don't have to wrap it up in clean linen for *me*!'

'When did I ever?'

'Never!' She smiled bitterly, remembering how once, long ago, she had let her love show and he had rejected her harshly. 'And I'm sorry to disappoint you after you've come all this way but you're out of luck,' she continued bravely. 'I'm coming, I'm bringing Davey with me and nobody can stop me!' As soon as she had said the words, she regretted them. They were more than a statement of intent, they were a challenge. She had just thrown away her last chance of being able to change her mind.

'In any case,' she continued tartly, 'I've an idea I'm mentioned in *Taid's* will; or is that your real reason for not wanting me there? Not delicacy but sheer spite? Ellis misbehaved herself so she mustn't benefit, and what she doesn't know about . . .'

'Since when have you ever found me dishonest?' He raised his eyebrows over narrowed eyes and his magnificently bold nose thinned as though there were a bad smell under it. 'There will be a few pieces of jewellery, I believe.' He eyed her sardonically and then let his eyes drift around the room, lingering on the old but still jewel-bright Aubusson carpet, the tall display cabinet of Meissen and Sèvres porcelain and the carefully tended pieces of genuine antique furniture. He looked back at her disdainfully. 'All this and you're still not satisfied!' he mocked while his heavy-lidded, slightly slanting dark eyes continued an assessment of his surroundings. 'Your late husband left you a fortune, but you still can't wait to get your greedy little fingers on a handful of seed pearls and garnets set in silver! You'd come all that way for such paltry stuff? *Duw annwyl*! Don't you already have enough?'

'*Taid* always said they'd be mine,' she broke in. 'They were promised and they'll help me remember him. Besides, they'd look funny on you.' Now she could laugh at him naturally. 'But I think such a long journey means there's something bigger at stake, more worth while than seed pearls and garnets set in silver. Do I get the west lodge as well? That also was promised. A place of my own where I could put down roots, that's what *Taid* said, and he prided himself on never breaking his promises.'

'Over my dead body!' His dark eyes glittered menacingly.

'Or maybe over mine if you don't control that temper of yours.' She winced away from him in mock fright and raised an eyebrow. 'Don't you know?' And at the tightness of his face, she broke into a genuine chuckle of triumph. 'No you don't,' she answered her own question with an ill-concealed titter. 'You're as much in the dark as I am! Whatever happened to that ducky little clerk in Williams, Jones, Jones and Powell, Solicitors; the one you were so—er—friendly with? Isn't she still whispering sweet nothings in your ear while you show her the way through the woods?'

His face relaxed into a smile which held a hint of sardonic triumph. 'You're behind the times, Ellis; she married the younger of the two Joneses. Now she *knows* the way through the woods!'

'And another redhead bit the dust!' she mourned, getting in another dig, but so obliquely that it went over his head. 'So you don't know any more than I do but I warn you. If the lodge is to be mine, you can't stop me living there. Me *and* Davey!' she added defiantly.

'It's been empty for several years; it's in no condition to be lived in.' The smile had gone from his face and his eyes were back to being bits of dark grey slate, hard and unrelenting, which made her more determined than ever.

'As soon as I know I have title,' she said it musingly, 'I'll *make* it fit to live in. You'd be surprised what money can do if you have enough of it, and I have! Meanwhile, we shall live with Aunt Vanno.'

'*My* aunt! She's only your foster-mother,' he reminded her, 'and she's getting on. Sixty-plus and not as hearty as she used to be. Do you think it would be a good thing, at her age, to land her with visitors, one of them a child, after all she's been through? She loved you and Gwenny equally even though Gwenny was her own child. I blame you for Gwenny's leaving home!'

'You think I encouraged her?' Ellis shook her head. 'I didn't, you know. You're being deliberately blind,

Gideon; you know as well as I do that *nobody* could stop Gwenny when she'd set her mind on something; and everything turned out well. Her mad—according to you—idea of being a photographic model wasn't so mad after all; I never thought it was. She has the face, the colouring and figure for it.'

Just for an instant, it was as though Gwenny were there in the room with them; tall and elegant, her creamy skin and red-gold hair glowing in the lamplight, long jade-green eyes sparkling with laughter or hard with purpose between dark lashes, and her mouth an enticing curve. Ellis felt a prickle of gooseflesh and banished the phantom. 'Instant success!' she continued mockingly. 'Just as I predicted. And now, she's in the States with her sights firmly fixed on the front cover of *Time* magazine.'

'It broke my aunt's heart.' He said it flatly. 'She's no longer the same woman.'

'I think you're exaggerating, but I'll decide about that when I see her.' Angry resolution kept her calm. 'Maybe she is and maybe she isn't. Maybe our visit will do her good, you never know, and it was she who invited me. A phone call in answer to my letter. If I think it's too much for her . . .'

'. . . you'll come back to London?'

'No,' she smiled at him sweetly. 'I'll find somewhere else to stay. There are any number of places. I could hire a caravan or better still one of those holiday cabins, which would suit Davey down to the ground. The fresh air will be good for him, it's what he needs after the dreadful winter we've had. Now,' she adopted her 'perfect hostess' manner. 'Before you go, what can I tempt you to; whisky? There's a very good single malt and I can safely recommend it. My late husband was something of a connoisseur.'

'*Cythraul*!' And at the lift of her chin, 'Yes! Devil! I wasn't swearing, just saying what you still are, what you've always been. A smooth-tongued, secretive little bitch out of hell, and the only thing you'll tempt me to is breaking your neck!'

'Manners,' she reproved him gently. 'It's not done to spurn my hospitality. Take a deep breath, sit down and stop losing your temper. Relax before your blood-pressure goes through the roof. I'll make you a soothing cup of tea.'

She didn't hurry over making the tea, she stayed in the kitchen and boiled the kettle three times before she judged the butterflies in her stomach had stopped fluttering their wings, and when at last she returned with a loaded tray, she smiled even more sweetly as she offered him his; without sugar or milk as he always drank it. He handled the thick pottery mug and raised an eyebrow.

'Is this the way you treat all visitors?'

'No.' She was sedate. 'Just you! It's your temper, you know, and I'm rather fond of this tea service. It's quite old and replacements are non-existent. I wouldn't like a piece to be smashed; it would spoil the set.'

'And you've done so well for yourself,' he sneered, but she nodded with a spurious gaiety.

'Yes, I have, haven't I? What you could call a meteoric rise to affluence. Just picture it.' She paused for a moment to add milk to her cup, stirred and sipped to nod approvingly before she continued in a light, airy manner which effectively concealed the irony behind her words.

'I was barely nineteen years old, straight off the mountain and all alone in this big, wicked city, with only a diploma from a second-rate secretarial college to recommend me. Then, here in this very house, I met the modern equivalent of the Good Fairy. He gave me my first job, temporary of course, but I fitted in so well! In no time at all, I was a permanent fixture.'

'Just as you did at Dyffryn,' he mocked. 'You've more wiles than a cat. The poor little orphan, a dear, sweet little child, rescued from God knows what fate by my impulsively romantic aunt. You were only nine years old but you knew, even then, who to go for. It took you less than a week to have my grandfather eating out of your little hand.'

'But I loved him at first sight.' She batted long, very dark, silky lashes and looked demure. 'And he loved me.'

'Oh yes,' he was sardonic. 'With your pale hair and big grey eyes, everybody loved you.'

'Everybody but you, Gideon,' and she curved her mouth into what she hoped was a sly smile. She would play the part he had allotted her, that of a scheming, rapacious woman. 'I couldn't con the infallible Gideon Llewellyn ap Gruffydd, could I? You saw through me straight away, didn't you?'

'No-o.' He said it slowly as if he was really thinking about it, and the hardness of his eyes softened into a gleam of wicked appreciation. 'Even when you were only nine years old, your brand of magic was very potent.'

'I bet you put the flag up when I left! And speaking of leaving,' she primmed her mouth, 'when you've finished your tea, I think you ought to; leave, I mean.

It's getting late, and I've my reputation to think of.'

'Your reputation?' He cocked a disbelieving eyebrow and his tone was bitterly ironic.

'No worse than some others I could mention,' she assured him with a bland sweetness which was belied by the gleam in her eyes. 'But you aren't fooled, are you, Gideon?' She smiled deprecatingly. 'And that's really all that matters. You give meaning to my existence; the one person who is sure he sees me clearly.'

Suddenly, she felt exhausted and, to cover her need to get away, she cocked her head at an imaginary noise and rose swiftly.

'Davey,' she explained, 'I'll have to go. You can see yourself out? Just slam the door behind you, it's self-locking. Goodnight, Gideon; see you at Dyffryn.'

CHAPTER TWO

ELLIS ran up the stairs as though the devil were at her heels, but once she reached the landing she forced herself to a stealthy tread. It had only been an excuse to get away, there had been no noise from Davey and she suspected Gideon knew that, but she could safely rely on his excellent party manners. In his own house, he might have followed her and continued the fight, but here, he would show a surface delicacy. She was safe, and all she had to do was wait.

She crept into Davey's room, seated herself on a small, button-back easy chair and closed her eyes while she waited. Gideon wouldn't slam the door either; well, not very hard, and the house was well built, almost sound-proof. She probably wouldn't hear him leave. For the first time, she regretted that Davey's bedroom overlooked the tiny scrap of garden at the back. If she had chosen a front-facing one for him, she would have been able to raise the blind and see Gideon leave. She shrugged and let her head rest against the chair-back, listening to the boy's soft, regular breathing while her mind slipped back in time to that night, over five years ago, when she'd opened the door of her small flat on a distraught but somehow defiant Gwenny. 'I'm having a baby.' Gwenny had said it baldly as soon as she had stepped over the threshold. 'I can't hide it any longer, so I can't model, and I've no money to speak of.

24

You'll have to help me, Ellis, for Mam's sake. I don't want her to know.'

'Of course I'll help,' Ellis had soothed as she had ushered Gwenny up the narrow hallway. 'You can stay here with me. It's not very big but you can have the bedroom and I'll take the divan in the living-room; it's quite comfortable, and don't worry about money, my job pays very well and I've saved quite a bit. Let's have a cup of tea and make some plans. The father . . . won't he . . .?'

'It's Gideon's,' Gwenny had said later when she was comfortably ensconced and sipping tea, 'damn him! But if he thinks I'll go whining to him for help, he's mistaken. He shan't ever know about it; I'd die sooner!'

'But Gideon would marry you, you know he would.' Ellis had tried a gentle remonstration, only to be met with a bitter laugh from her foster-sister.

'He asked me before, but I turned him down flat!' Gwenny was obdurate. 'Live in that dead-and-alive hole for the rest of my days? Not me, Ellis!' Abruptly, she changed the conversation. 'I saw a doctor this afternoon, he says I'm marginal for a legal abortion, but I can't . . . I'm too frightened. I'd rather have the baby! And there's nobody else I can go to, only you. Promise you won't tell Mam or Gideon, not ever. Promise, if anything happens to me, you'll look after the baby.' And Ellis had promised, cross her heart and hope to die, just as she had done when they were children.

Gwenny's plan had been simplicity itself. She would stay with Ellis until the baby was born, then decide what to do, and if things had remained simple and un-complicated, that was what would have happened; but things hadn't been that simple.

First, it hadn't been an easy pregnancy, nor was it an easy birth, and Ellis had taken so much time off work to be with Gwenny before the baby was born that Robert Blake, her employer, had demanded an explanation. It was a case of telling him—he had always been very understanding—or losing her job: one she liked, was happy doing and which paid well. She simply couldn't have afforded to lose it, not then.

Amazingly, Robert *had* understood; he was a slave-driver where work was concerned but children were his passion. And later, he had visited, and Gwenny was always better, less moody and strung up after those visits.

Then, barely a fortnight after Davey had been born, Gwenny had been wild with delight about an offer from a fashion photographer to go and work with him in the States, and Ellis had come home from work the same evening to find Davey yelling the place down and Gwenny packed up and gone.

There had been the obligatory note on the table of course. Gwenny didn't think she was cut out for motherhood . . . fame and fortune were within her grasp, she couldn't refuse the offer . . . Robert had said he was willing to adopt the baby . . . it was the best way and Ellis must get in touch with him straight away, he knew where to find her. All of which was little comfort to Ellis, who had grown devoted to the small scrap of humanity wailing in his makeshift cot.

She had known she couldn't keep him on her own, much as she wanted to, so she had made Davey's overdue bottle and when she had fed him, she had phoned Robert who had arrived at her door half an hour later with his plans already made.

Uninvited, he had read Gwenny's farewell note before he had bundled Ellis and the baby into his car and ferried them back to his house.

'I offered and Gwenny accepted; my solicitor's already looking at the legal angles. He can tie this up before Gwenny leaves for the States.' He had been firm and quite sure of himself. 'But if you don't like the idea, the best thing for you to do would be to contact Gwenny's mother or the child's father.'

'No!' Ellis could recall, even after all this time, how violent she had sounded and how sick she had felt. 'I promised Gwenny I wouldn't do that! I also promised her I'd look after him. I love him and I promised, but I can't think of any way.' There hadn't been a way until Robert had made his suggestion.

'You could marry me,' he had said wryly, almost hesitantly, as if he were afraid she would refuse. 'I love you, Ellis, as much as I can love anybody, but I know you don't love me and I wouldn't ask you for anything you're not willing to give. Marriage with me would solve most of your problems,' he'd argued reasonably, 'and in a way, you'd be doing me a favour. You've promised your foster-sister to look after Davey and I've always wanted a child, so together we could adopt him; he'd be our son.' His expression was wry. 'Silly, isn't it? You'd think any man could do a simple thing like father a child, but I can't! Discount the gossip you must have heard; that's the real reason my marriage ended in a divorce.'

'But it wouldn't be fair to you,' she had gulped, and Robert had given her one of his rare, sweet smiles.

'So what? Life's hardly ever fair, Ellis. We just have to make the best of it, get what we can out of it.'

'Make the best of it!' The words were ringing in her mind as she opened her eyes in the darkened room. A glance at her watch told her that only ten minutes had passed—so many memories, so little time—not enough to be sure Gideon had gone. She gave it another five before she crept out of the room and sidled down the stairs like a thief in the night to patter along the passage to the kitchen, where she switched on the kettle. She was just reaching for a mug and the jar of instant coffee when she felt rather than heard the door open behind her and Gideon's voice jeering at her from the doorway.

'Getting a child to sleep must be an exhausting business, Ellis!' She swung round on him. The short break had given her a chance to rebuild her courage and she felt nearly fit enough to cope with the devil himself —which was just about the same as coping with Gideon when he was in one of his forbidding moods. Think *beautiful* thoughts, she told herself; think about Robert! She willed her face into serenity.

'I thought you'd gone.' She said it with a cool, almost biting humour. 'So many calls on your time and not a minute to waste.'

'Not many.' He strode across the kitchen and stood towering over her. 'Be ready in the morning, you and—and the boy. I'll pick you up at nine.'

'His name's Davey,' she told him firmly. 'You needn't be afraid to say it, but no, I shan't accept your offer. I shall perhaps need transport while I'm at Dyffryn, so I shall take my own car. I know you would be more than willing to drive us anywhere we wanted to go,' she made the point with gentle irony, 'or even to hell, which is where you'd prefer to take us, but I don't much care for grudging charity or being beholden . . .'

'Mountain roads aren't made for your type of car!'

'Now he tells me!' She made it sound demure and a bit chastened, but the smile she gave him was pure wickedness. 'And after I've sold the Lotus, the Jag and the Ferrari and bought myself a nice little hatchback GTE. But the salesman said it would cope with anything, so I shall just have to give it a whirl.'

Gideon grunted in what she judged was pure fury and swung on his heel, heading for the front door. Like any good hostess, she trotted after him, even made motions of being about to help him on with his coat and grinned when he brushed her help aside. She was right, she *was* infectious, and he was afraid of catching something; perhaps an attack of civilised behaviour!

Still within the doorway, he stopped and rounded on her. 'You seem to know a bit about cars.' He made it sound like an accusation.

'Mmm,' she nodded serenely, although her insides felt like jelly and there was a queer hurting in her throat. 'I've had years of tuition from an expert. When he was younger, my late husband both designed and raced them. I'm sure he would have approved of my choice!' And quietly but definitely, she shut the door in his face to run upstairs swiftly just to make sure that the sound of voices in the hallway hadn't wakened Davey.

After contemplating his sleeping face, she looked at the photograph of the thin-faced, fair-headed man who had been first her employer and later her husband. She fancied there was an expression of approval on the pictured features. Robert had always appreciated her courage, and what he had liked to call her 'viper's tongue' had amused him.

But her phantom comfort didn't last long. It crept away again as she went down to the kitchen to make herself a sandwich and a pot of tea, leaving her full of doubt. Was she doing the right thing? Wouldn't it be easier, better to forget? Had she any right to interfere? She shook her head definitely at the teapot and put her hands around its fat body, seeking the warmth to take away the chill in her fingers.

Forgetting wasn't easy, in her case it was near impossible, and as for having the right; upstairs was a child with rights and she intended to see he got them even if it meant riding roughshod over all the narrow-minded hypocrisy in the world.

Somehow, she would establish Davey at Dyffryn; he belonged there. Besides, she wanted to go home, and home would never be this elegant little house in London. Home was with Vanno, high in the hills and overlooking a placid little river meandering through a steep-sided valley. Home was a clean wind with the tang of the sea on its breath. Home was where the heart was, and her heart was still at Dyffryn, with Vanno and Gideon. Laboriously, over the years, she had dug a deep hole in her mind, buried Gideon in it, covering him with the huge pile of her contempt; all of which should have killed her love. Perhaps it had. Surely it wasn't love which made you want to batter a man to death, stamp him into a bloody pulp?

Feeling a little better about everything, she buried her doubts deep and set about clearing out the fridge, pushing everything into a black plastic sack, save for the few items she would need for breakfast. After which she went upstairs, showered and scrambled herself into bed. But when she slept, it was to dream, not of Gideon but of Gwenny. Beautiful, charming, restless, wilful Gwenny with the sunlight making her hair gleam like a new-minted penny.

When she woke in the morning, she felt completely rested and fit for anything. She had taken the first, most difficult step. All the others would follow on as a matter of course, and the next step was to wake Davey and stand over him while he washed himself. He always forgot his ears!

But later, the doubts and hesitation were back in force, supplemented by a twinge of fear as, with Davey safely strapped in the back seat of the hatchback, she drew away from the kerb. Her rear offside mirror gave her a plain view of the shabby, work-a-day Land Rover which pulled out from where it was parked half-way down the street and accelerated to fall in behind her and follow her decorous progress towards the M1.

Anticipated as a simple journey from London to Middle Wales, the trip had all the makings of a disaster. The little hatchback was both nippy and powerful but Ellis cursed silently for not allowing herself enough time to become familiar with it. Added to this, she tended to be over-careful because of her precious passenger, who kept up a nerve-racking chant of all the nursery rhymes he knew by heart, demanding that she sing them with him.

But the main reason for her nervousness was the Land Rover and its eagle-eyed driver. They stuck behind her, matching her speed mile for mile; she knew she was being closely watched and it didn't improve her performance so she turned off at the Watford services to get a cup of coffee, which she hoped would steady her nerves.

That didn't help either. As she flicked her indicators and slewed on to the slip road, the Land Rover copied her manoeuvre as if she were towing it and not trying to lose it. It parked beside her but Gideon didn't get out, he just sat watching as she took Davey to the toilet and visited the cafeteria where she queued for coffee and fresh orange juice before bringing the child back to the car and strapping him into the back seat again.

Davey was quite happy with his juice; he was enjoying the novelty of this departure from his normal routine, and she leaned on the bonnet of the hatchback, drinking her coffee and feeling the April sun on her face until she felt some of the tension sliding away from her. Finally, draining the paper mug and gaining a little more confidence, she marched over to the waste disposal, tossed the container into its depths and marched back, stopping at the side of the Land Rover en route.

'*Must* you stick so closely on my tail?' she demanded sweetly. 'I keep thinking I'm towing you and it's very off-putting.'

'Escort duties.' Gideon opened his door, swung himself out of the driving-seat and came to lounge against the bonnet. 'Vanno's orders. I was to see you safely home.' He gave a snort of mirthless, abrasive laughter. 'My poor aunt; she thinks you can't look after yourself! That you're a poor, lone widow-woman struggling alone in the big city to bring up your child. For heaven's sake, when you get there—if you ever do, and by the quality of your driving, I very much doubt it—put her mind at rest on that, at least. She has enough to worry about without wasting her pity on you!'

'She already knows, I've told her often enough.' Ellis was indignant, she flushed and the vagrant colour in her cheeks made her grey eyes sparkle. 'I've explained my position to her. Why should she think . . .'

'Too many lies,' he was brief, 'and she has other worries.'

'Not about me!' Ellis interrupted fiercely. 'And I've never told her any lies!' And she hadn't! Maybe she hadn't always told all the truth but that had only been so that her foster mother shouldn't worry! 'I've married the most wonderful man.' She had put that in a letter and it had been the truth. Robert *had* been wonderful; kind, generous and—as he had so often said—with enough love and understanding for both of them. But time had taught her that such a one-sided bargain could never be fair; her fondness for him, her respect and gratitude, even their eventual lovemaking had been a poor return for all he had given her. She owed his memory a debt she would never be able to pay.

'We have the loveliest baby in the world.' She had written that as well, and it also had been the truth; Davey had been, still was a beautiful child! With her mouth open on a further protest, Gideon stopped her with a curt motion of his arm. She flinched visibly at the menace of it, only to be met with a further vitriolic outbust.

'Don't try those games on me, Ellis, they won't work, I've watched your performance for too long. You're not a bit afraid of me and I know how you can look like an abused angel almost at will. For my money, you've always been an ingratiating little opportunist, all take and no give, I only wish Vanno could see you with my eyes. Now put on your doting-mother expression—you've let it slip during the last five minutes—and get back to your car and your son before I wring that delicate little neck of yours and,' he added softly but with menace, 'drive carefully. If you're not used to the car, take your time. We've got all day, and I'll be right behind you.'

Ellis shook her head as if to rid herself of a nightmare, but it wouldn't go away. So much concentrated hate aimed at her was beyond her comprehension. She wasn't perfect, she had never pretended she was. She had her share of human weaknesses, a deep envy perhaps—when she had been younger—of the people who were safe and secure in a family circle, and she tended to be secretive. She certainly didn't spill out her woes to all and sundry, and then there was her temper. Mostly she kept that under control, but sometimes it spilled out in a frank and not always diplomatic fashion.

But as for the 'ingratiating opportunist' thing, it just wasn't so! An opportunist, yes; she didn't dispute that. Nearly everybody took advantage of opportunities, but she had worked hard for hers. She had sat over her school books when Gwenny had been out enjoying herself; crept up to the Plas in the evenings to practise on the typewriter in what *Taid* called his estate office. She had worked just as hard for the year she'd been at the secretarial college, worked even harder for Robert, but ingratiating, no; she'd never been that!

Gideon was treating her as if she were two-faced and poisonous, but then he always had. No, she forced the truth up from her memory. There had been a time, when she had first been brought to Plas Dyffryn; Gideon had been all right then. Stiff as a board and loftily superior, but she had only been nine years old to his twenty, so that was understandable. The rot had set in later, culminating when she had been sixteen and desperately in love with him. Just once, she had let it show and he had grown even more remote and suspicious.

With a little shrug, she turned away and went back to the car. The defiant swing of her slim hips sent the soft tweed of her skirt flirting about her legs and her chin was set obsinately high, but inside her was the old, familiar feeling of having been pounded into the ground with a steam-hammer. The sight of Davey and the warmth of his smile calmed her down a little. At least there was one person who loved and trusted her, even if he was only five years old. Somebody had told her, or perhaps she had read it somewhere, that very young children had infallible instincts.

'We going now?' He asked it hopefully, looking up from the picture of a bear he was colouring a lurid pink, and then added with a nod at Gideon who was swinging himself into the Land Rover, 'Nice man!' Which completely destroyed Ellis's belief in the infallible instinct of the very young!

Nearing the end of the journey, Ellis pointed out that there was still a little snow on the rounded tops of Cader Idris but Davey was not very impressed, despite the fact that she had detoured miles out of the way mainly to give him a sight of it. To him, a

mountain ought to be blinding white and conical like
the Matterhorn. She had also had other reasons for the
detour; a faint hope that this close to her destination,
she would shake the Land Rover off her tail. It had
been nerve-wracking to see it constantly behind her.
That, and Davey's small face, which was becoming
pinker by the minute and starting to wear an agonised
expression!

But when she drew up in Dolgellau, the Land Rover
slid gently into the empty parking space beside her
and Gideon rolled down his side window with a
scowl.

'Again! That's the second time since we passed
Shrewsbury.' He made it sound sinful, and her mouth
curved into a genuine smile as she unstrapped the
little boy and hauled him out.

'Yet again!' She chuckled. 'Children are like that,
they don't have much control over body fluids, you
know. They're always either wanting to restore them
or get rid of them. It's why we've had to stop so often.
Have a few kids of your own and you'll soon learn!'
Something about him changed, she couldn't put her
finger on it, but she seemed to feel a lessening of
tension, even a little warmth. Whatever it was, she
welcomed it and determined to do nothing to spoil it
while it lasted. She didn't suppose it would last that
long.

'Can't afford them,' he riposted.

'Oo—ooh, Gideon!' Her eyes sparkled with malice
as she headed Davey in the direction of the nearest
tea-place. 'I didn't know you were so mercenary!'

'We both are.' The Land Rover's door slammed and
he fell into step beside her, shortening his stride to

match hers. 'The only difference is that you've achieved your ambition. Do you want me to carry the boy?'

'You could ask him if he'd like that.' She was judicious. 'Remember, to him you're a stranger and he's been warned about strangers. If you swoop on him, he could be frightened.'

'Would you like a ride on my shoulder?' Gideon stooped and was at his most winning. It didn't get him anywhere!

'No, thank you. Ellis says I'm not to have rides with *anybody*!' Davey continued to stride out manfully but when they entered a teashop and, his needs attended to, he was safely ensconced at a table, he turned an interested gaze on Gideon. 'I'm Davey Blake. Who are you?'

'You can call me uncle.' Gideon let his eyelids fall and he was back to being harsh again, but in a winning way. 'I expect you've a lot of uncles, haven't you?' Ellis seethed and felt herself growing stiff with anger, but Davey saved the day.

'No,' he said positively. 'No uncles, no daddy, only Ellis.' He gave the matter some thought. 'I *did* have a daddy, but he's gone now. I've got an aunty,' he offered, before allowing his attention to be distracted by a glass of milk and a buttered scone.

'And that serves you right!' Ellis muttered as an aside at Gideon as she poured the tea, her face set in a smile so stiff she thought her features might be carved in stone. 'I thought you were being too good to be true! Anything like that, you can ask me straight out; there's no need to question an innocent child. I don't tell lies!'

'Aunty Vanno,' Davey added belatedly, pleased at remembering the detail. 'She's Ellis's really, but Ellis says I can share. D'you know my Aunty Vanno?'

'Mmm.' Gideon deftly buttered another scone and slid it on to Davey's plate while his eyes met and held Ellis's gaze. 'She's my aunty as well; I take care of her.' He added the verbal warning for Ellis's especial benefit.

'Why can't she take care of herself?' Davey's eyes surveyed him wonderingly. The idea of an incompetent adult was a new one, and he had difficulty in accepting it since his circle of acquaintance was limited to Ellis, the nursery school teachers and a dozen or so other children of his own age.

'She's an old lady,' Gideon explained and Davey nodded with dawning comprehension as he thought about it.

'You have to help her across the road so's she's not knocked down by a bus. Don't you have lollipop ladies where you live?'

'Finish your milk, Davey.' Ellis interrupted what could very well turn into a long and rambling discussion. 'We have to be on our way or we'll be late.'

'Finished.' Davey crammed the last piece of scone into his mouth and spoke through the crumbs as he slid from his chair. 'Bye bye.' He was politely dismissive and Ellis couldn't resist a smile, albeit a mocking one.

'That puts you in your place nicely, doesn't it,' she murmured derisively. 'Whatever happened to that charm for which you were so famous?'

'All knocked out of me.' His eyes grew deadly as she fumbled in her purse for money—he had paid for their lunch at Shrewsbury—and his fingers closed over her wrist, forcing hers to stillness. 'My treat.' He was sardonic and she could feel the strength and purpose of those fingers, even think they were bruising her, and when she had settled Davey in the car and slid into the driver's seat, she examined her wrist. She wouldn't have been surprised if his grip had left weals but her skin was quite unmarked.

So, Gideon still had his fierce pride; he hadn't learned, as she had, that pride could be too expensive.

Half an hour later, she turned the nose of the car into the narrow lane which ran nowhere except to her foster-mother's house and, further on, to a gate and a footpath which wandered away into the surrounding hills. The Land Rover followed her every move but she ignored it as best she could. Gideon was apparently set on keeping tabs on her. Distrust was a cankerous thing, and he seemed so eaten up with it that he was set on blighting everything, even a reunion between herself and the woman she loved most in the world.

She had been away for only a bit over seven years, Ellis told herself. Nothing could have changed that much in so little a time; yet the lane was definitely narrower and her foster-mother's house—a Victorian anachronism in shiny red brick in an area where most buildings were of stone and slate—looked a lot smaller than she remembered. But Vanno hadn't changed! A tall, thin woman with an abundance of grey hair and a plain face lit to beauty by a pair of dark, passionate eyes, she marched down the front garden path between borders of daffodils and was there at the side of the hatchback before Gideon had brought the Land Rover to a halt.

'Ellis,' she said in a voice which made music out of the word. 'You haven't changed a bit, still too thin but it's lovely to see you and after all this time. Pity it's such a sad occasion.' It was the only concession she made to the reason for Ellis's visit, and only a slight moistness in the dark eyes showed the sorrow her father's death had been to her.

'Vanno.' Ellis was out of the car and hurling herself against her foster-mother's meagre bosom. There were old arms about her, a quick, brisk hug, the touch of a still soft cheek against hers before she was abandoned and the older woman had the car door open and was fumbling with Davey's straps.

'There's my lovely.' She turned back to Ellis with Davey firmly in her arms. 'Not a bit like you, Ellis. I suppose he takes after his father, but he's a fine boy. There's a good, long back here; he'll make a big man.'

Ellis's heart plummeted, almost stopped for a second, and she had to swallow convulsively before she could speak. Was it all in her imagination, that faint resemblance she sometimes saw so plainly? It must be, or her foster-mother would have spotted it. There was nothing wrong with Vanno's eyes, they were as keen as a hawk's.

Maybe you only saw what you wanted to see. Ellis summoned up a smile, artificial at first, but it swiftly became real and rather rueful. Vanno should have married early, not late, and to a lusty young man, not the ageing, sickly organist she had known all her life. Then, she might have had half a dozen little rascals instead of only Gwenny, her one ewe-lamb, and Ellis, the orphan she had fostered. She loved children and children loved her.

Ellis spared a glance at Gideon, who was descending leisurely from the Land Rover with a tight, mirthless smile twisting his lips as he watched Davey being set on his feet to stump up the garden path with his hand firmly tucked in his Aunt Vanno's, the late afternoon sunlight making a pale halo of his fair curls. He was being made much of and he liked it, his face was one broad beam of delight.

'You've lost him, Ellis.' Gideon was wry. 'It'll break her heart if you take him away from her now.'

Ellis presented him with her public face, quiet, smooth and unreadable, while inside she felt her heart pounding. 'Did you think I didn't know how it would be?' she said maliciously. 'Why else would I have come!'

'For a handful of seed pearls and garnets set in silver,' he mocked, and she felt her temper slipping away but she grasped it firmly, controlling it. She wouldn't be pushed into losing it, not yet.

'And the west lodge,' she said defiantly. 'If it's mine. It'd be a good place for Davey to grow up in, and Vanno would be happy enough with that arrangement. We'd be close enough to see her every day.'

'Ellis, this child needs cleaning up.' Vanno's voice broke in; carrying clearly, it seemed to reverberate from every hillside surrounding them. 'Don't stand gossiping, plenty of time for that later. Have Gideon bring in your cases. He may as well stay for tea.'

And Gideon was still there hours later, sitting in front of the kitchen fire and talking to Vanno when Ellis came down from putting Davey to bed. They were to share the big, twin-bedded room at the top of the stairs, the one she had shared with Gwenny when they were children, and Davey, tired but still excited by all the unusual goings on, had taken a long time to settle in a strange bed.

CHAPTER THREE

GIDEON made motions of leaving. 'Get a coat and walk with me a little way,' he said, and it wasn't anything as polite as a suggestion. He had never made suggestions to her, only given orders. It seemed he was still doing that. 'It isn't too cold,' he added as her mouth opened on an excuse, and the set of his jaw was formidable. 'The fresh air and exercise will be good for you after driving all day. You'll sleep better.'

'That's right,' Vanno added her mite. 'You look pale, Ellis. You never did have much colour, but now you've none at all.' Her voice slipped from Cheltenham Ladies to a soft Welsh lilt. 'Like a little ghost you are, *cariad*, but never mind, we'll soon put that right.'

Ellis herself had a few things to put right. That, she told herself, was why she was shrugging into a sheepskin jacket and leaving the warm kitchen to step out into the gathering dusk. It was like walking beside a living threat, but just this once she had to do it.

'You seem to have changed your mind about our staying here.' She snapped it out as soon as they were out of earshot of the house. 'Last night, you implied you didn't want us here.'

She felt rather than heard his weariness. 'I've driven all day as well, Ellis. I'm as tired as you are. Too tired to fight with you, but there are things I have to know and the first is, do you intend to make trouble?'

'Why should I do that?' The growing darkness hid the set of her small chin but her low voice with its hint of challenge reeked of obstinacy. 'When did I ever? So that leaves it up to you! You leave me alone, let me have what's mine without a fight and I'll be as peaceful as a cooing dove.'

'The boy?' He pressed the question. 'I'd like to know more about him. Was your late husband his father?'

'What a question to ask, but, since you press me, the answer is no!' She kept her voice flat and uninterested.

'Did he know that, your husband?'

'Of course.' She shrugged and summoned up a bit of strength to fight back. 'Not that it has anything to do with you, only with Robert, and, as he knew and accepted, what gives you the right to ask personal questions? I'm only answering them because I've nothing to hide.' She said it out of sheer bravado and with her fingers crossed. Of course she had something to hide, who hadn't? And hide it she would. 'Any more questions?' she asked pertly.

'No point in asking them.' He stood tall and still in the rapidly falling darkness. 'You're too good at telling lies, you've even improved on past performance. If I didn't know better . . . ' He shrugged.

'You'd believe me?' Her little snort of amusement was quite genuine. 'You find it hard to believe that Robert could accept me with another man's child and give us both his name and his love. I'll excuse your disbelief; you didn't know Robert and you'd never have understood him in a million years.'

'Which all sounds very high-minded and romantic,' he broke in harshly. 'I should have remembered you were good enough to pull the wool over *Taid's* eyes and Vanno's, but you don't fool me, my girl.' All the lilt had gone from his voice; it was toneless and uncompromising. 'Or perhaps you're not trying very hard, and why should you? You've nothing to gain from me. I've nothing to give, only a warning: I won't have Vanno made unhappy!'

'So?' She shrugged and turned on her heel. She was getting nowhere. She had hidden nothing, the pieces of the jigsaw were all laid out for him to see, but he was too deep in the groove to put them together properly. His hand on her arm pulled her back.

'You can leave when I've finished, Ellis, and I'm not finished yet, not by a long way!' Under the grim, too quiet surface she could feel the anger simmering in him, and suddenly she was frightened. She wanted to run back to Vanno, but the hand holding her showed no sign of relaxing its grip.

'I know you, Ellis,' he growled softly, and that made it worse. Shouting wouldn't have worried her but this quiet grimness terrified her. 'You're a vulture,' he continued in a harsh whisper. 'When you'd driven off Gwenny and picked Vanno and *Taid* clean, you went to London where you soon found another poor fool ready to be meat for you. You married him and, on your own admission, foisted another man's child on him. Now, you're a wealthy widow, but still you're not content. You're back here for whatever else you can get!'

It was his sheer blindness that drove her to it. She raised her free hand and slapped his face, hard, only slightly gratified by his jerk of surprise. 'You can condemn when you *know*!' she spat before she pulled herself together and became icily calm. 'And you don't *know* anything!' Angrily, she turned on her heel and would have stamped off but she tripped over a tangle of exposed tree roots and went sprawling into the muddy ditch.

'Stupid.' Gideon bent over her and extended a hand to help pull her to her feet. 'Why don't you wear sensible shoes? Are those the ones you wore for driving? No wonder you made such a mess of it.'

'That's right!' She squealed it furiously, feelings of hesitation and guilt buried under a thick layer of angry humiliation. 'Don't bother to ask if I've hurt myself, just criticise my shoes. I didn't want to come walking with you anyway, so it's all your fault if I've broken my ankle!'

'And have you?'

'How do I know?' She gave an exasperated grunt. 'I haven't tried to stand on it yet!' Tentatively, she lowered her foot to the ground and put her weight on it. Nothing drastic happened, no shooting pains and no scrunching of broken bones, only the conviction she had collected most of the mud in the ditch on her hands and face, not to mention the front of her sheepskin jacket.

'No lasting damage,' she admitted grudgingly, attempting a mopping-up operation with a small lace-trimmed handkerchief which wasn't equal to the job, and she began to feel ill-used. 'I bet you wished that on me; you've hated me for years. I don't know what I've ever done to deserve it, it must be all in your mind, but I stopped caring about that a long time ago.'

'All in my mind,' he interrupted savagely. 'Oh, no, my dear, and don't play the hard-done-by orphan with me. You may reduce Vanno to tears of pity for you, left alone in the world to bring up a child. You may even impress her with your undoubted ability, but then, you always were clever and very, very efficient. Anything you did, you did well, but you neither impress me nor make me pity you. There's nothing in you, not a single human feeling but greed!'

'What a character assassination!' The shock of his attack had left her numb and she spoke in a cool, remote little voice. She even managed a little thread of amusement to run through the words. 'So that's what you think! But tell me, what am I after now? Not the west lodge, surely? According to you, I'm more rapacious than that!'

'That's what puzzles me, Ellis.' He admitted it frustratedly. 'What *are* you after?'

'A way through the woods, perhaps,' she answered him wearily. All her strength seemed to have been used up; she felt weak, tired to death and almost defenceless. The old catchphrase had come into her mind and she had said it for something to say. After all, it was no use telling him that, apart from paying her last respects to an old man whom she had loved very much she was really here for Davey's sake. Every child had a right to his proper place.

There was the old story that Truth lived at the bottom of a well, quite unable to be got-at! Maybe it did, but confirmation was what she really needed. Not that Gwenny would ever have lied to her . . .!

'Only a way through the woods?' Gideon's manner lightened immediately and she could have slain him on the spot for his complete misunderstanding. 'Is that all?' he murmured. 'You should have said before.' She felt the warning prickle and the cold flowing through her once more. 'Any other woman, Ellis,' he continued jeeringly, 'and I'd have had scruples, but not with you. I think you were born knowing the game backwards!'

His dark head swooped and she felt first the chill of his cheek against her own and then the even colder chill of his mouth on hers. But the chill didn't last. It grew into warmth and a sense of coming home. She thought it could grow warm enough to burst into flames. Flames which would scorch her because this fire was all she had ever wanted, even though she would burn away to ashes and be destroyed for ever.

It was silly how you could believe you had outgrown a young girl's love. Sillier still to have labelled it youthful infatuation when all the time you had known it was there forever. Ellis still loves Gideon! She thought that could very well be inscribed on her tombstone! A death-blow, and she'd bleed forever from it if she lived to be a hundred.

The knowledge had only come with the first flicker of the blaze which threatened to consume her, and it hadn't even shocked her. She knew now, now, when it was years too late, that it had never been fear she had felt for this man. The fear had been all for herself because, deep down, she had known that she was vulnerable, that a few kind words could reduce her to a grovelling heap.

It was a frustrating, one-sided love, but now she knew it had never died, only slept a while; she would go on loving him forever. A bleak prospect because it was one of those things which could never lead anywhere, and something inside her rebelled at the thought. It wasn't the same for him, he was only using her, and she started to fight the steely grip of his hand and arm; fought the hard pressure of his lips on hers.

If she gave an inch it would be tantamount to defeat, and she wasn't in the business of self-destruction, but her struggles seemed to have no effect. She was being humiliated and the humiliation went on and on; Gideon was enjoying himself, almost revelling in the contest. Abruptly, she stopped fighting, got a hold on herself and went quite limp and lifeless. Let him discover for himself he wasn't getting anywhere. It would get through eventually.

And eventually, it did. He raised his head with a grunt of disgust—possibly at himself, although she doubted that—she was set on her feet, there was nothing holding her and all that was left was the pain of her bruised and swollen lips. That and the new knowledge of her vulnerability which frightened her. She waited until she was sure her voice would be normal, not even indignant. There was no sense in exposing herself to more danger.

'Not *those* woods!' She said it frostily and, though it cost her a lot in self-possession, she turned away from him on her heel and sauntered back along the lane with a straight back, her head held high and a defiant swing of her slim hips and shoulders.

But there was no defiance in her heart, only a great, cold emptiness. Gideon's kiss had been an insult, a blatant, sexual attack with no spark of tenderness in it, only force and a desire to dominate, to punish. She had refused that domination and she should be waving a flag or beating a drum, so why wasn't she? If only he had been different, if everything had been different . . . If only . . .!

The table had been cleared when Ellis entered the kitchen, but the dirty dishes and pots were still stacked in the scullery. 'I thought I might break the rule of a lifetime and leave them till morning,' her foster-mother explained guiltily, raising her head from her everlasting knitting—she gave it all away as birthday or Christmas presents and any excess went to the Chapel sales of work. 'I didn't want to make too much noise,' she added, 'not before Davey was properly asleep. The old cistern rumbles when it's filling.'

'He's only a light sleeper for the first hour or so.' Ellis forced a tinny-sounding laugh. Already she was beginning to feel better, even able to be proud of herself for the impression of impregnability she had left with Gideon; she hoped it was stamped on his mind in letters of fire. Once, long ago, she might have been a pushover for him, but not any more!

'After that,' she continued, leaving the scullery door open so that Vanno could hear her above the running of the taps as she filled the sink, 'you might as well try to rouse the dead. Have you heard from Gwenny recently?'

'Not recently.' Vanno snorted her disapproval before making excuses. 'I get a telephone call now and then. She doesn't have much spare time nowadays. She's modelling for a fashion magazine, but she'll have told you about that.'

Ellis called back from the sink where she was up to her elbows in detergent froth. 'Yes. It sounded very glamorous and time-consuming. It could explain why I haven't heard from her for ages. Does she know about *Taid?*'

Vanno abandoned her knitting and came to stand in the doorway. 'I told her he was failing the last time she phoned. When he died, I telegraphed her. She asked me to do that.'

'Then you've done everything you can.' Ellis scrubbed busily at the pile of plates. 'You'll hear from her soon; a bit late, I expect, but when was she ever on time?'

Even with her head lowered over the sink she could hear Vanno's faint sigh. 'I can't help worrying about her, Ellis. She's so impetuous, you never know what she's going to do next. And I never did like the idea of her modelling. Old-fashioned of me, I suppose.'

Ellis stacked the last plate in the drainer, emptied the sink and rinsed and dried her hands. The routine gave her time to arrange her face in a bright smile before she returned to the kitchen. 'Very old-fashioned,' she agreed. 'Times have changed, modelling's quite respectable. It's not as if she were a Page Three Topless, and the pay's good. Besides, Gwenny's an extrovert, she's beautiful and she knows it. It would be a sin to hide her light under a bushel.'

'I suppose you're right.' Her foster-mother was comforted if not convinced, and she dropped the subject in favour of a more immediate matter. 'Funeral tomorrow. I hope it doesn't rain, though I suppose it will,' she mourned, 'all over my new black hat!'

Ellis snuggled down gratefully between her foster-mother's lavender-scented sheets. She needed sleep, the whole day had been exhausting, but sleep wouldn't come. In the other single bed, Davey slept the sleep of childhood, quiet and uncomplicated, and she wished, oh, how she wished she could be a child again, with no bigger worry than whether Vanno would spot the carefully mended tear in her blazer.

Methodically, she recapped on each incident of the day. Had she handled everything with the correct amount of *savoir faire?* At last she came to the conclusion that, having kept her temper under great provocation, she had done the best she could. She had been cool enough with Gideon, even after his assault; and assault was the only word for it.

Had he been hoping to frighten her off? It would be just like him to use his rampant maleness as a threat; the brute was uncivilised. She drew a little comfort from the thought that he hadn't succeeded, and a wry satisfaction that her fleeting response to his cavalier treatment had gone unnoticed.

But it wasn't going to happen again; she wouldn't allow it, she couldn't stand it! She would make damn certain that in future he'd have no chance to get that close to her. With him she might weaken, and once he discovered that—she closed her eyes despairingly—he mustn't ever discover it! At this point she slipped into an uneasy sleep . . .

Morning came with Davey bouncing heartily on the bottom of her bed, and she faced it, wan and weary, and with a dull feeling of acceptance. Her marriage to Robert had been a cosy, comfortable thing. Born of necessity and nourished by propinquity and mutual respect, it had grown into a sweet, very gentle loving because Robert had been a lovable man.

But now, she knew about passion; not the girlish thing that had hit her at sixteen. That had been bad enough, but this was infinitely worse. She ached with it, but nothing could come of it so it had to be hidden. The effort paled her face and made her eyes dull. Davey on the other hand was full of beans; for him it was another special day and had to be treated as such.

'My *best* shirt,' he reminded her as she laid out his clothes on the bathroom stool. 'Mind my manners,' he repeated his instructions parrot-fashion. 'Eat all my breakfus, keep myself clean, wipe my feet on the mat and no shouting 'cause this is a sad O-K-shun!'

'That's a big word for a little man,' she teased him and left him to his ablutions; she would inspect his ears later.

'You're sure Davey will be all right?' Breakfast was over and Vanno called it from the kitchen. Ellis answered from the scullery where she was coping with the tray of dirty breakfast dishes. Vanno hated washing up; she would have to be talked into having a dishwasher.

'You're worrying about nothing again,' she soothed, putting the tray down on the draining-board and turning on the hot tap. 'He's five years old, not a baby any longer. He'll behave!'

'We'll have another hot drink before we go,' her foster-mother said decisively. 'Look at that mist. We'll get wetter than if it was raining. Ellis, that black suit makes you look like a stick; you're too thin. There's not a spare scrap of flesh on you, but I suppose that's the boy. A nice little lad, but he keeps you on your toes, I expect. Does he favour his father? I can't see anything of you in his face.'

It was the same question again, just phrased a bit differently, and Ellis washed the last plate three times, glad she had her back to her foster-mother. Deceiving

Gideon was one thing, she gloried in it and lived for
the moment of triumph when she could look him in
the eye and tell him the truth. But deceiving Vanno?
She hadn't expected to be doing that!

When she was sure her voice would be cool and
composed, she put the plate in the rack and turned
from the sink with her smile in place as usual.

'Yes,' she said quietly. 'I've always thought he takes
after his father.' And to steer her foster-mother away
from what could be a tender subject, 'Let's have some
coffee with a drop of something in it to keep us warm.
Rum would be nice but not too much, or everybody in
chapel will know what we've been up to.'

Ellis sighed with relief as she left the dining-room at
Plas Dyffryn—the solicitor had taken over the room for
the reading of the will—and she gave Gideon an
agonised look, accompanied by a perceptible shudder
as he held the door open for her.

The rambling old house was no longer the warm,
comfortable place she remembered; there had been no
fires lit, nothing had been polished and it was drab
and as cold as a tomb. Her fleece-lined coat had
protected her from the worst as she'd stood on the
bleak hillside but the damp mist seemed to have percolated into the fabric so that she had dispensed with it
when they'd entered the Plas. During the solicitor's
long-drawn-out performance over *Taid's* will, she had
shivered in her lightweight black city suit. Even her
feet were frozen where the damp had seeped through
the thin soles of her shoes. Now the chill was
spreading through her so that she wanted to hurry
away, back to Vanno's warm, cheerful kitchen and out

of all this decaying grandeur and gloom.

She refused Gideon's offer of cake or sandwiches, also the ritual glass of sherry; instead she poured herself a cup of tea and drank it thirstily. Even that was only lukewarm, and she hoped Davey wasn't prancing about outside and catching a chill.

The seed pearl and garnet-studded silver necklace and earrings were hers, just as *Taid* had promised; he had never broken a promise to anybody and he hadn't broken the one about the west lodge either, but she would have given all of it, plus every penny she had in the world, just to have him back and feel the warmth of his old smile one more time.

The lodge; she would put any repairs in hand straight away and she and Davey would live there, whether Gideon liked it or not. As for the jewellery, maybe one day Gideon would have a dark-haired, dark-eyed daughter who would like to wear it for her first grown-up party.

She found that thought so painful that she was almost sick, so that she abandoned her teacup and fled to the main door, only to find Gideon there before her, his hand on the latch, waiting to open it for her. His face was inscrutable, and her eyes were so full of tears that she didn't trust herself to speak nor even to nod. She was hurrying to catch up with Vanno; he wouldn't dare make a scene in front of his aunt. Her lips twisted bitterly as she changed her mind. Of course he would make a scene, if he felt like it, Vanno or no Vanno! The thought lent wings to her feet, but he was still beside her when she hurtled through the door and on to the top of the steps which led down to the terrace.

'Wait, I want to talk to you.' He made it grim.

'Can't be bothered just now, leave it till later.' She adopted a spurious calm. 'Where's Davey? I want to collect him and get back home. Vanno's upset, she needs company. She's bound to feel the loss, even if she doesn't show it. You've sent her off with Davey, I suppose,' she hazarded peremptorily. 'Hoping to get me alone so you can show a few more strong-arm tactics? If so, they won't work any better than they've done before. I'm staying and that's final!'

'As you wish.' His voice was bland and her surprise showed, she even felt the blood warm in her cheeks so that she looked away from him, back through the open doorway to where the solicitor was making inroads on the plate of sandwiches she had spurned and helping himself to sherry; pecking and slurping away like a carrion crow. She recalled the man's far from pleasant treatment of herself, as if because she wasn't a real member of the family, only a foster-child and from South Wales at that, she was the dregs of creation. She sniffed angrily.

'I believe Mr Cledwyn Jones doesn't approve of my being here or being a legatee.' It helped to have something else to be angry about. 'I suppose it's because I'm not a real member of the Gruffydd family. You'd better be careful, Gideon,' she added nastily. 'Don't come too close to me, it won't do for you to mingle with the common herd.'

'I'll survive.' As her irritation increased, so he appeared to grow calmer. 'And I'm coming with you to Vanno's.' She looked her surprise and his mouth went wry. 'Where else can I expect to get a meal? *Taid's* housekeeper—er—no,' he corrected himself, '*my* housekeeper's one of the sensitive type. She's been snivelling so hard she's given herself a headache and taken to her bed. I'm hungry.' He tugged at her arm. 'Let's go and pick up Davey, and when we've had lunch we'll park him with Vanno while you and I go for a walk and some serious business discussion.'

'More blackmail?' She lifted an eyebrow. 'More bullying? You've got a nerve, Gideon! I wouldn't talk business with you, not without an impartial witness or a tape recorder in my hand so that I had a record of every word. You trample on little people like me. And what do you mean, pick up Davey? Is he still here? I thought you said . . .'

'You're getting muddled, *cariad*.' He shook his head gravely. 'I didn't say anything, you didn't give me a chance; you jumped to conclusions, as usual. It was *you* who said I'd sent him home with Vanno! Actually, I sent him off with young Idris Evans; they've gone down to the *"hen"* where my collie bitch has a litter. I've more or less promised Davey he can have one of the pups; depending on the whim of his dear Mama, of course. And by the way,' his fingers increased their pressure on her arm, 'regarding my trampling on little people like you, I promise not to trample too heavily.'

'A qualified promise . . . is no promise at all.' Obeying the pressure of his hand, she walked briskly, almost running along the long frontage of the Plas. It was too damp and cold to dawdle, and her words came out in between gasps of breath in the moist, mist-laden air as she gave examples. 'I'll do it . . . if I have time! I'll be there . . . if I can make it! And now, I'll not trample . . . too heavily! Worthless!' She made a small sound of disgust.

'You look quite charming when you wrinkle your nose like that.' Gideon sounded almost humorous but there was no humour in his grasp of her arm; it hadn't decreased in pressure by one iota. 'It reminds me of when you were a little girl. You once found a dead mouse in your pocket, but you didn't scream or faint. You made your mouth smile but there was murder in your eyes!'

'You put it there!' she accused flatly. 'The mouse and the murder!'

Inside the long stone-walled, stone-flagged, single-storeyed outhouse, Davey was jubilant while the older boy—Idris, she supposed, she didn't remember him, he'd have been little more than a toddler when she left—looked relieved. Davey scrambled up from a pile of straw and came rushing towards her with a small black and white pup in his arms.

'Look, Ellis,' he chanted, 'Uncle Gideon said I could have one, I want this one. He chose me! I didn't touch him, he crawled straight to me, didn't he, Idris? I can have him, can't I?' He paused for breath and then started again. 'Ellis, why does Idris call this the "hen" place, there's no chickens.'

' "*Hen*" is a Welsh word, Davey.' Gideon gave her no chance to explain. 'It means old. This is the oldest part of the house; long, long ago, it *was* the house, all the rest hadn't been built.'

'The Elizabethan gable, the Jacobean staircase, the Georgian bit, plus that ghastly Victorian conservatory where nothing will grow!' Ellis became waspish in a low mutter which didn't reach Davey's ears. She was shivering. In her haste to get out of the house, she had forgotten to pick up her coat, and the dampness was chilling her to the bone. But it didn't get her anywhere, Gideon simply ignored her derogatory comments to go on speaking to Davey.

'Is that the pup you want?' and, at Davey's violent nod, 'Then, perhaps later, when it's older and can leave its mother, you can have him. But only if Ellis says you may.'

'That's right!' Ellis snarled the aside. 'Putting the onus on me! Look at it! It's going to be huge and hairy and it'll fill the place up with pups and fleas!' But Davey wasn't listening. There were few windows in the old building, they were all very small and his smile of content was like a beacon in the gloom.

'*My* dog, Ellis,' he chanted. 'It chose me. It loves me. See, it's licking my face. Can I hold it a bit longer?'

'Five minutes only.' Gideon was uncaring of his good black suit as he knelt on the straw-strewn flags and poked an experimental finger in the pup's tummy. He grinned up at Ellis.

'No pups, this is a dog,' he pronounced. 'No trouble for you when you get back to London.'

The older boy scrambled to his feet with an air of relief and a murmured, '*Rydw i'n mynd i'r y ti,*' and Ellis smiled at him as she seated herself reluctantly on a spare batten of straw and watched him vanish through the door at the speed of light. That much she could understand; Idris was going home. Nursemaiding a lively five-year-old could be very wearying, as she had reason to know. Meanwhile, there was Gideon's last remark to counter, and she gave him a saintly, long-suffering smile.

'But we are not going back to London, Gideon. Had you forgotten that, or are you indulging still in wishful thinking?'

He raised a dark eyebrow at her, it rose in a demonic peak so that he looked quite satanic. 'There's no place for you here, Ellis,' he said, and his tone was wintry so that she had to conceal a shiver. 'You or the boy. I want you gone, and as soon as possible. Better for everybody that way, especially Vanno. She still has a few illusions about you, I want her to keep them.'

'You're sure you're saying this for Vanno's sake?' Ellis's lips twisted in wry self-derision as she identified the tight knot of pain which his flat statement had given her. Not kicked in the teeth but in the stomach; she wasn't important enough for her wishes even to be considered, and the pain wasn't going to go away. It was the hungry pain of being rejected by one particular man, this man, and she thought that, now she had identified it, she would be hungry for him for the rest of her life. Maybe this was just a little of how Gwenny had felt: used and rejected. So much worse than her own experience; she had only been rejected!

CHAPTER FOUR

NEVER before had Ellis felt so miserable, but in the midst of her confusion one thought kept her steady. Cover up! Give Gideon an inch and he'd take the lot, show one sign of weakness and he'd massacre her. A desire to do a bit of hurting of her own kept her face blank and almost expressionless, while her voice surprised her by being quite steady, almost a triumphant jeer.

'It wouldn't have anything to do with you personally?'

'Only that Vanno's a much-loved aunt and a member of my family,' he snarled. 'I won't have her upset! She loves and trusts you.'

'My, my!' Ellis's grim little smile was as wintry as his own. 'A nice appeal to my better nature, but it's not going to work. I've run out of the milk of human kindness and I've made all the sacrifices I'm going to. From here on in, it's me first and anything over is mine as well. You said the lodge was in a bad state.'

'It'd cost.' He shrugged, but there was a feral gleam in his eyes. 'You'd need a surveyor, a builder and time. It would take months to bring it up to your standard.'

'Now, I'm sure you're exaggerating.' She smiled at him sweetly and became businesslike. 'Two rooms to start with,' she snapped. Hadn't Robert coached her for hours on end to concentrate on one thing at a time, to distinguish between information and misinformation? 'The kitchen and a bedroom, that shouldn't take long or cost more than I can afford. We could move in as soon as they're ready. Or,' she slanted her eyes at him suspiciously, 'are you going to fix it so that I can't get a local builder?'

'With all the money you have?' He grinned at her mockingly, but there was a savage glitter in his eyes. 'We may be Welsh but we're not fools. Your cheque would be as good as cash on the nail, and the Welsh have been poor too long!'

'And when the work's done?' She was still suspicious. 'We move in. What then? Do you send for Plaid Cymru or the Welsh Nationalists to harass us or burn the place down about our ears?'

'How could I?' Gideon raised an eyebrow and looked innocent. 'You're Ellis Blake, born Ellis Morgan, as Welsh as they come although you don't speak the language. Who could deny you the right to live in Wales?'

'You're trying to,' she reminded him softly, 'but you aren't succeeding, although I suppose you'll make everything as difficult as possible just to discourage me.'

'I've had no success so far,' he reminded her just as Davey's plaintive, 'I'm hungry, Ellis,' hit her ears and she struggled to her feet, drawing a deep breath.

'Of course you are, love, it's a long time since breakfast.' She said it brightly. 'Put your pup back with his mam—he's much too young to leave her yet—and we'll go straight back to Aunt Vanno's. I expect she'll have a meal ready.'

Davey was reluctant; he was too young to understand why he couldn't have his puppy straight away. His small face became mutinous and he turned large, dark eyes on Gideon in a mute appeal. It didn't work, and Ellis turned her head aside to conceal a bitter smile. Davey's first lesson and she knew exactly how he felt. No aid from that quarter! Finally, he did as he was bid and scampered out of the door, but Gideon held her arm, delaying her while his hand smoothed down over her back and as she jerked away from his touch, he smiled nastily.

'Just brushing straw from your skirt, Ellis. You've changed quite a lot. I can remember when you were a bag of bones, but now there's a bit of shape to you. Did you love him, Ellis? Did he love you, your husband? Is that why you married him?' he asked it harshly. 'Or was it only for the security he could give you?'

It was a loaded question, and double-barrelled so that, whichever part of it she answered, she would be in the wrong. But hadn't it always been that way? The name of the game had ever been 'put Ellis in the wrong'. Delicately, she slid out of it.

'Did I love Robert, you mean?' She looked him straight in the eyes and let a reminiscent little smile touch her mouth. 'Yes, by my standards, I did. Loving somebody means understanding them, accepting them as they are and not trying to change them.'

'And of course, it wasn't hard.' He glared at her and the fugitive smile on her lips widened into mockery as she thought she detected frustration in his next remark. 'What woman would find fault with a man who could surround her with every luxury?'

'Oh, luxury.' She blinked at him cat-like in the weak

sunlight which had struggled through the mist to find a gap in the wooden planks of the door. 'That hasn't anything to do with money or possessions, Gideon. Not to me!'

'How *do* you do it?' he marvelled, still with the bitter twist about his mouth. 'Say all the right things at the right moment?'

'Easily,' she assured him without showing a trace of the pain he was inflicting on her. 'Nowadays, I just say what I think! I've learned to get my values in the correct order.'

'And you learned to do that so quickly.' His hand was on her shoulder, pushing her through the low doorway, and she stepped out into the weak, watery sunlight which was displacing the mist, following Davey's sturdy little form as it marched away from her. Was that an omen, a warning that she mustn't become too possessive?

The frontage of the Plas stretched ahead of them and she determined to count off twenty more steps along the terrace before she answered Gideon's nasty little barbed remark. She took a deep breath to calm herself and deliberately avoided being anything but practical and sensible.

'I *had* to learn quickly, a matter of survival.' She shrugged and grimaced. 'When Vanno first brought me here, luxury meant childish things, like having nice things to eat, soft pillows on my bed, fresh underwear and a clean dress every morning and Vanno promising me that, if I ate my porridge, I'd grow up to be a big, strong girl. All the little things most other children take for granted. Now I know better. Vanno feather-bedded me a bit, but I learned very quickly when I was out in the world on my own. I had to grow up in a hurry.'

'And your present definition of luxury?' Gideon was giving a good imitation of a terrier at a rat-hole. She thought he was trying to put her down or catch her out, and she couldn't understand why. A conflict of personalities, she supposed. They had always been like oil and water.

'Robert needed me, and now Davey needs me.' She shrugged and eyed him suspiciously as they followed the child back along the frontage to the main door. 'To me, that's luxury! Nobody ever needed me before.'

All the cars and mourners had gone by the time they reached the end of the terrace. She hadn't brought her own car, preferring to go with Vanno in the big black limousine provided, and only Gideon's serviceable Land Rover stood waiting. Grasping Davey's small hand in her own, she swung round on her tormentor.

'We can walk, it isn't far,' she said firmly.

'Show some sense, Ellis.' Gideon's voice had the familiar rasp. 'It's starting to rain again, the boy's tired and hungry and in that state a mile's more than he can manage, even if it is all downhill. You'll end up carrying him.'

'You think I couldn't?' She lifted her chin, but all it got her was another sardonic smile.

'Oh, I'm sure you could. You're bloody-minded enough for anything.' He tossed Davey, squealing with delight, into the back seat and strapped him in before he opened the door for her. 'In! Do you need any help?' And as she struggled with a high step, high heels and a pencil-slim skirt, his hands were about her waist and she was dumped on the seat like a parcel of groceries.

Vanno was looking strained when they arrived in the

kitchen and her eyes were suspiciously moist, but she summoned a smile and was her usual brusque self to them. Ellis knew the brusqueness was only a front to cover the sense of loss, so she accepted a scolding with an understanding smile.

'Keeping that child out all this time in the wet! Ellis, I thought better of you. He'll be damp and chilled to the bone. Take him upstairs at once and pop him in a bath to warm him up before you change his clothes and don't be long, lunch is spoiling. And as for you, Gideon; I suppose you've invited yourself for a meal. In your shoes I'd get rid of that useless housekeeper. I can't think why *Tad* ever employed her.'

Gideon shrugged. 'We both know the reason, *modryb.*' His eyes slid to Ellis who was on her hands and knees, removing Davey's damp and muddy shoes. 'Your *Tad,* my *Taid* never could resist a pretty female, be she nine or ninety; especially one with a sob-story sad enough to break your heart. But the lady's leaving at the end of the week and I was thinking, perhaps you'd like to take her place.'

'Me! Go back to live in that mausoleum? Better you get rid of the place and live here with me.' Vanno showed little sign of sympathy or family feeling for the Plas as she snorted, 'At least you'd be warm and well fed.'

'As you know, I had my eye on the west lodge,' he slanted a glance at Ellis, still on her knees and struggling with Davey's outer clothing, 'but *Taid* decided otherwise. It now belongs to Ellis and she plans to do it up and live there herself.'

'Ellis and that child alone in the lodge, miles from anywhere,' Vanno sniffed. 'I'd never rest peacefully in my bed. Talk her out of such a mad idea, *nai bach;* I'd say nothing if she had a man at her side.'

'Perhaps she'll take pity on me and have me as a lodger, *modryb.'* His eyes glittered savagely.

'And have every tongue between here and Dyffryn wagging?' It came out with a snort of disapproval. 'Yes, I know I'm being old-fashioned but . . .'

Davey's muddy shoes removed and dumped in the scullery for attention later, Ellis grabbed his hand and towed him out of the kitchen. He went unwillingly and as they reached the foot of the stairs, he shrilled a piercing protest.

'I'm hungry, Ellis. Not going to bed!'

'Who said anything about bed?' Ellis wrinkled her nose at him. 'You're going into a bath.'

'But I'm not dirty!' His conviction wavered as she opened one of his clenched little fists and made a face at the grime in it. 'Not *very* dirty,' he added apologetically. 'I fell over.'

'I know,' Ellis shook her head, 'but it'll come off easier in the bath and besides, it'll warm you. Food'll be ready by the time you're tidied up. In you go.' She pushed him into the bathroom, turned the bath taps on and stripped off the remainder of his clothes while the bath filled. 'There you are.' She tested the water and lowered him into it, tossing in a handful of lavender-scented bath-crystals for good measure. 'You scrub up while I fetch you some clean things, and don't forget your face and ears!'

Outside, on the landing, she heard the discussion drifting up from the kitchen and sheer curiosity overcame her normal good manners so that she paused to listen. Her foster-mother had a carrying voice—she was active on a great many committees—and Gideon's deeper tones were quite distinct.

'Too much for you, *annwyl modryb*,' he was saying. 'A whole houseful. At your time of life you want a bit of peace,' and his aunt's reply came scornfully.

'I'm not in my dotage yet! Besides, I like the company and Ellis would be here to help me; I've been on my own too long.'

'No,' his reply came sternly. Gideon was putting on his head-of-the-family act. 'Maybe for a few weeks, but no longer. I think my idea's the best.'

'You can't be serious! You know I'd never permit that.' Aunt Vanno was crisp. 'You'd get Ellis talked about!'

'Why? We're practically related; she's almost a cousin. One I've known since she was a child, and she's no longer a young, single girl but a widow with a little son.' He was speaking clearly and with annoying coolness, and in English! Ellis credited him with eyes in the back of his head or an ability to see round corners and decided she was probably intended to hear and understand every word, otherwise he would have switched over to Welsh. It made her feel better about listening in to a private conversation.

'You knew, everybody knows I was going to put the lodge in order and live in it myself,' he continued forcefully. 'The rest of the estate's showing a healthy profit but the Plas is a millstone round my neck. The constant repairs alone eat money I could put to a better use. The *"hen"* is a listed building, it *has* to be kept but the rest could be pulled down or . . . there's your suggestion . . .'

'You're really considering that?' Vanno sounded

pleased.

'It's one way,' Ellis could almost see Gideon's shrug, 'but the lodge has to be made fit to live in before I can make any real plans. It would be handier for me than your house; nearer the bottom of the valley. However, there's Ellis, but we'll cross that bridge when we come to it.'

Ellis scurried off into the bedroom before she heard any more, to spend a frantic five minutes collecting fresh clothes for Davey and give her cheeks a chance to cool down before she hauled him from the bath.

When they reached the kitchen, Gideon and his aunt were still squabbling but amicably.

'You heard that, Ellis?' Without turning his head, Gideon knew that Ellis and Davey had rejoined them. 'It seems Vanno's stuck with a houseful.'

'I heard some.' Swiftly, she conquered the flutter in her stomach and as she saw the self-satisfied smile, almost a smirk, on his face, she bit her lip. He used people, and now he was using his own aunt to get rid of herself and Davey, but she wouldn't let him get away with it, not so easily.

'I think,' she made it placid and matter-of-fact as she padded Davey's chair with a cushion and seated him on it, 'if you can't live at the Plas—and without a housekeeper it would be practically impossible—Vanno's invitation is the best you'll get. You can accept it, you know; neither Davey nor I will disturb you. We'll be out most of the time.'

'Of course you will,' he broke in with a wolfish smile. 'I'll see to that. We can't have aunty overtiring herself.'

Ellis flushed and choked on an epithet as she spooned potatoes on to Davey's plate. Her foster-mother was in the scullery but Davey's ears were waggling, and he had a child's ability to remember and repeat any unsuitable word. During the late lunch, Gideon—very slyly, Ellis thought—turned the conversation in the direction she least wished it to go. 'You've heard from Gwenny recently, *modryb?*' he asked his aunt.

'No, not since I phoned her just before her *Taid* died.' Mention of her beloved daughter made Vanno glum. 'I was telling Ellis about it; she understands these things better than I do. She says modelling's quite respectable and very well paid, but will you look at these,' she took a sheaf of much handled, full-page magazine illustrations from a dresser drawer. 'Whatever have they done to her? See that,' she pointed disparagingly at the top one, 'that isn't our Gwenny!'

'But it's very good.' Ellis looked at the photograph, a head and shoulders in full colour of Gwenny in a dramatic black hat, and she allowed her lips to curve in an appreciative smile. 'As you say, it isn't our Gwenny, but you're supposed to look at the hat. Fashion's the name of the game. I like this one.' She leafed through the little pile to find a full-length Gwenny in a jade-silk evening gown which matched her eye make-up perfectly. 'I'd be tempted to buy something like that for myself,' she admitted ruefully, 'if I were six inches taller.'

Vanno showed signs of being mollified—which was what Ellis had been aiming for—and her gaunt face broke into a smile, rather a smug one. 'It wouldn't suit you, *cariad*. You couldn't carry it off. I'll say that for Gwenny, she always looks good in whatever she wears.'

'Have you heard from her recently, Ellis?' Gideon

caught her eye and his eyebrow rose in a mute query.

'Not for a while,' she answered in a colourless little voice. 'Not for more than two years,' she could have said in perfect truth, but what was the use? Out of sight, out of mind, but shattered illusions had a way of twisting in the wounds they made; they left a dull ache. She knew from her own experience that it was better to live in a whole dream than to live with the broken shards of one. One could be happy living in a dream, there was no reality about it.

She stole a sideways glance at Gideon; did Gwenny write to him? Useless to ask the question, he had always covered up for his cousin. She knew that if she asked, she wouldn't get an answer and there wasn't a trace of surprise on his face. Did he already know Gwenny hadn't written to her? Probably he did, thought Ellis viciously, and on his express order! As if he felt her glance, he turned to her with his charming smile going full blast and deliberately changed the subject.

'Vanno and I have arranged everything. We all stay here with her for the time being and everybody's happy.' He said it, but he didn't mean it. She thought Gideon had no intention of her ever being happy, not if he had anything to do with it. Her suspicion was confirmed the next morning, when, coming downstairs at six to make Vanno a cup of tea, Ellis caught Gideon siphoning petrol from the tank of her hatchback. Careless of her hastily tied dressing-gown over an extremely unseductive cotton nightdress, she stormed out of the house and into the yard to face him belligerently.

'Why pinch my petrol?' she demanded caustically. 'You know I only put a couple of gallons in at

Shrewsbury. I've just enough left to get down to the garage in Dyffryn. And don't say the Land Rover's dry; it's a diesel and you've got oceans of the stuff!'

'No good for Vanno's electric generator,' he answered blandly and looked at her with withering scorn. 'They haven't brought the electricity this far yet, so how else d'you think she lights the place and runs the freezer?' He dribbled the last few drops from the pipe into a five-gallon can, sloshed it about and grimaced. 'Not much, as you said, but it'll keep her going for a day or two.' He looked down at her triumphantly as if he were daring her to make a fuss. 'I knew you wouldn't mind. Generous to the last drop of her blood or, in this case, petrol; that's our Ellis!'

'I do mind, I mind very much,' she grumbled angrily. 'I was going to take Davey down to the coast today.'

'Then your loss is my gain.' Gideon wasn't in the least perturbed. Her crossness didn't affect him one bit, he simply ignored it. 'When I've packed up a few things at the Plas, I'll bring them down here, dump them and take you myself.'

'You can spare the time?' She was acid and immediately regretted it; she would have to be a lot more diplomatic if they were to live in the same house, if only for a short while. Shivering in the chill morning air, she dragged her dressing-gown more closely about her and Gideon noticed. As usual he noticed everything!

'Inside with you, *cariad,* before you catch a chill. What are you doing down this early?'

'Making tea,' she shrugged, turning to re-enter the house. 'Vanno will be waking soon, I'm taking her a cup in bed. Do you want one?'

'Please.' He said it politely and she was struck by the

warmth of his smile, as if she had done something right for once and had to be thanked for it. It wouldn't last, of course; it never did.

She made the tea, took a cup up to her foster-mother and returned to sit opposite him at the kitchen table, searching for the right words and keeping her fingers crossed that she found them. 'You really meant it about pulling down the Plas? You weren't joking?'

'Not on so serious a subject,' he said. 'I'd flatten the whole lot if I could. You've been listening at keyholes,' he accused, and she shook her head aggravatingly.

'No! You were speaking quite loudly, in English. I assumed I was meant to hear. You can pull down part of the Plas if you want to?'

'It mightn't come to that.' Gideon tilted his chair and looked sardonic. 'A while ago, Vanno put me in touch with a charity who want a place to put their overflow of youngsters. They offered to take the Plas off my hands and at least the old place would be cared for. I've been toying with the idea.'

'Not as drastic as demolition,' said Ellis comfortingly, and he shrugged again.

'There are three choices for me.' He ticked them and their disadvantages off on his fingers. 'One: pull the place down but it would cost to clear the site. Two: give it to the charity people for use as a home for children, but I'd have to insist they were strictly overseen, especially at lambing time. Three: marry a rich wife, if she'd have me.' His mouth went wry as if there were a bitter taste on his tongue. 'Do you know where I could find one?'

'If you really want to keep the Plas, I know of a rich widow.' What demon had prompted her, she could never say, but the words escaped her almost without effort. And yet they *had* to be said, and it had needed far less courage than she had supposed to say them. This was the solution she had been looking for, and it would be just and equitable. It was only right that Davey should be accepted here. Gideon drained his cup and set it down carefully in the saucer before he raised an enquiring eyebrow at her. 'Now there's a managing little woman,' he marvelled. 'Coming up pat with the answer to all my problems. But the widow would need to be very rich.'

How she did it she didn't know. Pride, she supposed, made her look him straight in the eye. 'She is!' she said it flatly and felt the chill settle in her stomach so that she shivered again. 'Filthy rich!' she added wryly with a bitter taste on her tongue.

A sardonic smile tilted Gideon's mouth and his eyelids fell until his eyes were almost hidden; two glittering slits beneath his long lashes. 'Anybody I know?' he enquired silkily.

Just for a second, she hesitated while she manufactured a soft, mocking little chuckle and let it escape in what she hoped wasn't too shrill a tone.

'The only filthy rich widow both of us know, of course!' She was shocked at her own temerity but outwardly nothing showed. She told herself that these were days of equality. That men and women were supposed to have equal opportunities, equal rights, and after all, she hadn't actually proposed, only hinted. A hint she could always laugh off.

Just at the moment though, she was in an agony of suspense, waiting for his answer. The sudden idea was so right, it would solve everything, and she stuffed her hands into the pockets of her robe so that their trembling wouldn't be observed. She managed another idle shrug and clung grimly to her self-control.

'Of course,' she continued crisply with a crackle of breaking ice on her tongue—or was it her heart that was breaking?—'if you have any objections regarding birth and breeding—I know how proud you are of your own—we'll say no more about it!'

'The first proposal I've ever received,' he murmured as the shuttered look melted away from his face to be replaced by the ghost of a mocking smile, 'and all the advantages seem to be on my side. But what would *you* get out of it, Ellis?'

Her eyes slid to the window and she gazed wistfully at the hills, brown with a faint tinge of green on their lower slopes. Vaguely soothed, she withdrew her hands from her pockets and her fingers began to play a game with the sugar bowl, pushing it with the handle of her teaspoon until it would sit exactly in the centre of a printed wreath of flowers on the tablecloth. What *would* she get out of it?

'A home where I want to live,' she said steadily, 'and peace to live in it, I hope. Also a father for Davey.'

'You forget something, Ellis.' He moved like a striking hawk; one moment he was sitting opposite her and the next, he was behind her chair, lifting her out of it and swinging her round to face him. She lowered her eyelids so as not to see his face but she could feel his eyes burning with a cold flame. 'You're offering to buy me, and I believe in giving full value for money!'

'You can always refuse.' She raised her lids and her

grey eyes glittered like silver but her attempt at a shrug failed. She felt threatened and tried to cover it with an apt quote. 'If you can't stand the heat, get out of the kitchen.'

He picked her up on it straight away. 'Oh, I can stand the heat, Ellis. The question is, can you?' The fingers of his free hand found her chin and pushed it up until she was almost sure her neck would snap. It was a painful position and she was held in it while his eyes roved over her face insolently. 'Not bad.' He said it softly, very much as if he were commenting on the points of an animal. 'Good bone, but fleshed a little thinly; needs feeding up. Bit of a wild look in the eye,' he added thoughtfully.

'*You* are not buying me.' She brought it out in a painful whisper; her stretched neck made talking difficult.

'But you have just offered to buy *me*!' The fingers pushed her chin up a further centimetre. 'An arrangement which could cost me more than my freedom, so I have to be sure the stock is sound, although,' he paused and his mouth curved into a savage smile, 'I forgot. There's the boy upstairs, a good example of your breeding ability. Let's test your temperament.'

She watched dizzily as his face drew nearer to hers, closer until it blotted out the whole world, became her whole world and she gulped as his mouth fastened on hers. There was only a blatant, harsh demand in the contact and she closed her eyes on tears of savage disappointment. To him it meant nothing but she hurt so badly; she wanted to hurt back, and if he hadn't reminded her of Davey, of her aim in life, she would have bitten him!

She shouldn't have started this! She should have known he would be insulted and return the insult with interest. Oh, well, she relaxed and let the punishment continue, enjoying it in a queer, self-immolating way without a thought for Davey. There was nothing gentle in him, his mouth woke only animal responses, she could feel them as her mouth was invaded and his tongue probed deeply. Her free hand fumbled at the neck of her robe, trying to cover her hardening breasts.

Dizzily, she was aware as he lifted his head and through the thundering in her ears, she heard his voice. Unfortunately, it was still flat and hard, he hadn't been affected at all.

'Not a bad response, and quite amenable to discipline,' he pronounced evilly. 'You still want to stay in the hot kitchen, Ellis?'

'Y-yes,' she mumbled as she slid back into her chair, trying for a bit of composure, and as her self-confidence reasserted itself, 'it *was* my idea!'

'But you'll have a plan for release when the heat's too great?' She looked up to find him gazing at her thoughtfully. 'A quiet divorce, such as you arranged for your late husband and his ex-wife?'

'Robert's divorce?' Ellis's grey eyes looked straight into Gideon's dark ones and the softness was all gone from her. So he wasn't immune to gossip; she had thought he would be above that! A pity he had got it all wrong, and for a fleeting moment she puzzled her brain about his source of misinformation. 'How like you to bring that up!' She gave an exaggerated sigh. 'But there's more than enough money to compensate for any little weakness in my character. And money's what this is all about. You wouldn't touch me with a barge-pole if I didn't have enough, and to spare!'

'Temper!' he reproved her. 'And I intend to do more than touch you, Ellis. What about our own children?'

In that simple question he defined the limits of a relationship and it brought the blood to her face, flushing her pale cheeks, but now was no time for false modesty.

'They'd take precedence.' Having gone so far, said so much, she felt a desperate need to protect what was left of her dignity. 'Davey has a trust fund, he'd need nothing from you except help in growing up. But I'd want him treated as one of the family, no different from any other children we might have,' she added defiantly.

'As you were treated yourself.'

'Mmm,' she nodded. 'I was given time to put out a few roots. I'd like to have that for Davey.' And she settled back into a silence of near-nervous exhaustion. Holding up her end of the conversation had cost her a lot in terms of pride. The future she had offered might cost her even more. But the future was a long way off; it was the present which was bothering her, and how she would be answered. It had all gone too far now for her to brush it aside as a sick sort of joke.

CHAPTER FIVE

IT surprised Ellis when the answer came almost at once, as though Gideon had done some lightning sum in his head and come up with an advantageous answer. She'd been expecting either a storm of mocking laughter, beneath which she would die a little; or for him to take his time, deliberate while he figured out all the angles before he decided to put his neck in the noose she had offered.

Instead, there was movement; her chin was released and a hard, strong arm came about her narrow shoulders so that the companionable warmth of it seeping into the nervous chill of her body almost made her weep.

At that moment, she knew she'd bought a man! Not his heart or his soul, just his body, and she wondered if that would ever be enough.

'We'll wait till the lodge is ready.' He said it matter-of-factly as if everything was settled. She supposed it was, but she wondered how much this was going to cost her. Not in terms of money—she had never bothered about that very much—but self-respect.

Already, she felt almost a complete loss of self-confidence; she had proposed marriage to a man she loved but who neither loved nor wanted her. She hadn't grovelled about it, just treated it as though it were a business deal, but it had been hard going and the effort had left her feeling very low. She was sinfully proud of her own integrity; would she ever be able to be proud of herself again?

'That'll give us time to get used to each other.' Lost in a miasma of gloom, she heard Gideon's voice, calm and definite as if he were quite used to having offers of marriage tossed his way. 'Until then,' he continued, 'I'd prefer you not to tell Vanno of our arrangement, I'll do that at the proper time. A quiet wedding, I think. You agree?'

'Oh, much better that way,' she said, tasting the bitterness. 'Vanno's a bit romantic, I doubt she'd understand a purely business deal; besides, it'll give you time for second thoughts!'

'And time also for you to change your mind.' Gideon was sardonic.

'The arrangement will suit me very well, so I shan't.' Ellis's soft mouth became stubborn. All she wished to do was make it perfectly plain that there was no sentiment involved. He probably thought she would be a pushover for the 'now let's go to bed' routine and he had to be disabused. 'I told you,' she continued in a bleak little voice, 'what roots I have are here, I've always thought of this as home and it'll be a good place for Davey to grow up in.' Abruptly, she changed the subject. 'This tea's gone cold.' Her small hands enfolded the pot and she shook her head. 'Too cold for Vanno. I'll have to make a fresh pot. Do you want another cup?'

'Mmm.' He nodded with a smile which wasn't entirely free of malice. 'Good practice for you, *cariad*, and do you think you could fix me some breakfast? I've a field to plough this morning, and I'll need an early start if I'm to finish in time to take you and Davey out this afternoon.

'No need.' Ellis spoke wearily, as though she had already put in a hard day's work. 'We don't need you with us, I know the road to Ynyslas. Follow the river to Machynlleth, turn left at the clock and turn right at Tre'rddol.'

'But you sound tired already.' He broke in on her traffic directions. 'And in any case, your petrol tank is empty. I haven't time to get it filled this morning and I'm damned if I'll let you use my Land Rover. It's all the transport I have, and your driving . . .'

'I was taught by one of the best . . .' she broke in furiously.

'I don't care if you were taught by Jackie Stewart himself,' he snarled back at her. 'You're not driving my Land Rover, especially not with Davey as a passenger. I value his life, if you don't!'

The sense of that silenced her. Davey was too precious to risk while she fought with an unfamilar vehicle on roads she remembered only vaguely but she wasn't going to be too meek.

'Have it your way,' she grumbled crossly as she marched into the scullery to refill the kettle and empty the teapot. 'I wouldn't be seen dead driving the damn thing.' Her voice rose to an indignant squeal as she turned on the tap and shouted over the noise of running water, 'It's only fit for the scrapheap!'

The dunes at Ynyslas gave Ellis a bit of cover from the spring wind, although it was stiff enough to spray her face with stinging particles of sand and she could taste the salty grit between her teeth. On either side of the

Dovey valley, the mountains stretched back into the distance, mauve and brown against the sky and smoothly rounded by the millions of years they had stood there. Glyndwr had marched his men across those mountains, his 'Way' was still remembered although nothing of him remained now but his parliament house in Machynlleth, not even the knowledge of how he had died or where he was buried. Ellis wished she also could sink into oblivion and cursed the stupid pig-headedness which was driving her. But Glyndwr had always claimed to be a magician, whereas she had no magical powers.

Ynyslas, at the mouth of the Dovey estuary, was a Nature Reserve, complete with sturdy, rustic picnic tables and benches, and Gideon had brought them here in the Land Rover, with Llew his border collie, so that Davey could see what his pup would be like when it grew up. Vanno had hustled a flask of tea and sufficient food for an army into her old-fashioned wicker picnic basket and sent them off with strict instructions not to let Davey overtire himself or eat too much ice-cream.

The little boy had been warned away from both the wide curve of the Dovey estuary on one side of the spit of sand and dunes which was Ynyslas, and the waters of Cardigan Bay on the other. Both were dangerous when the tide was coming in; the incoming sea bored forcefully up the estuary and swiftly covered the huge expanse of sand. But Gideon had timed the outing well, it was low tide, there was no danger and the little boy, with the dunes to climb, the wide flatness of estuary sand to run about on and Llew to watch over him, was enjoying himself enormously.

'He'll get tired soon.' Gideon watched Ellis's agonised

face as Davey fell over for the umpteenth time. 'Don't worry so about him, Ellis; he's strong and healthy, he can take a tumble in his stride.' He sounded so consoling that Ellis desperately wanted to get away from the feeling of togetherness which insisted on creeping up on her when she wasn't looking.

'No hurry,' she shrugged. 'We've still a lot of things to discuss and I prefer Davey at a safe distance. He's at the stage when he repeats everything he hears without knowing what he's saying. I'd like to straighten out the money side of our agreement in private, if you don't mind.'

'Money's so important to you?' He slid down, flat on his back, and linked his hands under his head. Like that, she had an upside down view of his face which put her into a quandary. Right way up, she had difficulty in knowing what he was thinking; upside down, it was impossible.

'We wouldn't be talking like this if I didn't have it,' she said flatly and without any expression. In her position, she couldn't afford to wax lyrical about the virtues of love on a shoestring. 'Besides,' she went on smoothly, 'if anything happened to me, you wouldn't want to be left floundering.'

'As your mother was left floundering.' He raised an eyebrow as her eyes widened with shock. 'Yes, I know! Vanno had the bare bones of the story when she fostered you. How your father died early, how your mother couldn't face life without him. But you're not weak, Ellis. Whatever happened, you'd cope. You managed with Davey, didn't you, and it couldn't have been easy.'

'It wasn't.' She put the money affairs to one side—

they could be talked out later—and recalled the days when Davey was a small, very new baby and Gwenny had been completely uninterested. Her smile, if it could be called a smile, was wry. Nobody had ever known about those nights when she couldn't sleep and the days when she couldn't eat for worrying about how she was going to manage when Gwenny went back to work. It had taken Robert to solve that one for her. 'Until I married Robert, that is,' she said. 'After that, it was all plain sailing.'

'Robert loved you?'

'Yes,' she answered him tranquilly, 'we loved each other.' Not a crashing torrent of passion, she could have added, but something peaceful and very, very steady. Robert had been such an easy person to understand; just thinking about him made her feel calmer, stronger. 'But I still worked for him,' she added with a dry little chuckle. 'We were used to each other; he didn't want the trouble of training a new secretary and a temp would only have done the typing.'

'A racing driver needing a secretary?'

'He'd been retired from racing for quite a while,' she shrugged. 'He'd tried his hand at writing a book to pass the time. It wasn't a bestseller, but his publisher liked his style and asked for another. After that, writing became an obsession with him.'

'About cars and racing, I suppose?' Gideon was prodding her with a quiet question every time she stopped talking. Subconsciously, she admired his technique while she concentrated on her answers. Robert and his writing were safe ground, so she could afford to let her tongue wag a little as long as it didn't wag about Davey.

'I read quite a bit but I don't recall anything of that kind by Robert Blake,' Gideon added. That elicited a soft chuckle from her.

'Nothing much to do with motor-racing after the first book.' She crinkled her nose in amusement. 'He wrote crime novels and he called himself Blake Roberts. He was a sort of Dick Francis on wheels instead of horses. But it all needed a lot of research, and that and the typing was my department. It was a bit like being the junior partner in a business. Robert arranged everything for me: meetings with all sorts of professional people; solicitors, bankers, chemists, accountants, photographic and computer experts. I did the leg-work.'

'A bit of a slave driver . . .' He slipped it in as she paused for breath and, as usual, any criticism of Robert made her cross. She owed him so much, she couldn't bear to hear him criticised.

'Nothing of the sort!' She snorted disdainfully. 'Simply a perfectionist.'

'He kept you busy?' Again there was a little prod to start her talking again. She didn't mind that; it spurred her to be extra careful there was no mention of Gwenny.

'I suppose I'd better explain,' she shrugged. 'Because of Davey, I'd had to take time off and the work had piled up.' She gave Gideon an uncomplicated smile. 'Robert always hated wasting time. We decided to marry; he had a housekeeper who'd keep her eye on Davey between feeds while I caught up with the backlog of work. It was as simple as that.'

'It didn't bother you that you'd broken up his previous marriage?' The interjection spurred her to wrath and almost demolished her innate caution.

'Nonsense,' she almost spat at him. 'I don't know where you had that idea, it's completely wrong and all I can think is that somebody's done a good job of character-assassination; and at long range too! How a stupid story like that could have percolated this far is beyond me. I didn't break up any marriage; he and his wife had been divorced for at least ten years and she'd remarried long before I went to work for him. The dates are checkable, if you won't take my word for it!'

'And he gave up racing . . .'

'That, too, was before my time,' she broke in hotly. 'When he knew his reflexes were no longer quick enough.'

'But your marriage didn't last long.' Again that insinuating thrust, as if in some way or another *she* had been responsible for Robert's death. As he held her responsible for Gwenny leaving home and coming to London; for *Taid* leaving her the lodge, as he seemed to hold her responsible for anything and everything which didn't please him! She drew in a hard breath and lifted her face to look him straight in the eye. Robert had always said she was too quiet. He had advised her not to pull her punches.

'I know you don't have a very high opinion of me, but you can't blame me for that! she said calmly. 'I could hardly organise a dense fog on the M1, or the jack-knifed articulated lorry he ran into,' she said bleakly. 'So, he liked driving! Maybe he wasn't good enough to race any more but he was still a superb driver. If he crashed it was because he couldn't do anything else. If there'd been the least chance of getting out of it alive, he'd have taken it. He wasn't exactly old, and he had everything to live for!' She bit her lip hard to stop any tears or further talk and she turned her head to yell at Davey that it was time to eat.

Davey came running, accompanied by the dog, and they both flung themselves down, panting and scattering sand everywhere. The dog lay watching Gideon but Davey, with the perception of childhood, took one look at Ellis, scrambled to his feet and launched his sturdy little body at Gideon; small fists battering, knees pummelling and only his soft, canvas shoes preventing him getting in a good kick. Red-faced, he yelled, his treble pipe rising to a fierce screech.

'You've made my Ellis cry,' he accused Gideon. 'I don't like you any more!'

Gideon held the small tempest off at arm's length while he examined its small, flushed face before turning to Ellis.

'Call the child off, girl, before he hurts himself.' He was laconic as he controlled a furious Davey.

'Let him go,' she told Gideon abruptly and then, more soothingly to the child, 'It's all right, Davey. Nobody's hurt me, the wind blew some sand in my eyes, that's all.' Davey's struggles stopped abruptly and he hung in Gideon's hands like a puppet with no strings.

'Truly?' He wanted to be satisfied but wasn't, not quite.

'Truly!' She nodded at him and watched as his face resumed its normal hue. 'You don't have to fight for me, I haven't been hurt.'

'I wouldn't hurt your Ellis, Davey.' Gideon looked suitably downcast, making it sound oh, so kind, and she ground her teeth. Pulling his charm on a child

too young to distinguish between truth and simulation!
And her hands were tied: Davey mustn't get a bad
impression of Gideon; a boy should look up to the man
who was going to be—the idea brought a fugitive smile
to her lips—his father.

But the child nodded seriously as he was set down on
his feet. His frown disappeared, to be replaced with a
look of sympathy and some forgiving.

'Ellis has a sore spot and you mustn't touch it,' he
explained gravely. 'You have to be very careful, 'cos
nobody knows where it is. It keeps changing places,' he
added.

'Why don't you call her Mummy?' Gideon asked
lazily, and Ellis groaned as Davey showed all the signs
of lapsing into a confidential mood.

'I've seen *real* mummies,' he confided in a loud
whisper. 'Ellis took me one day when it was raining.
They were all dead and wrapped in dirty bangdijez!
Nasty!' He gave a convincing shudder. 'I like "Ellis"
better, don't you?'

Ellis didn't want to hear Gideon's answer so she
appealed to the animated—and always empty—
stomach which was Davey by opening the picnic basket
and running an eye over its contents.

'Milk or orange juice; beef or ham roll?' she offered to
stop any more infant revelations.

'A walk before bed?' The evening meal was over and
Ellis had bustled round, clearing the table and washing
the dishes to the accompaniment of the swift, liquid
Welsh that flowed back and forth between Vanno and
her nephew. She hadn't understood more than one
word in a hundred but she hadn't felt shut out. It was a

soothing language to listen to, and the sudden question in English startled her.

Gideon wasn't really asking, not even suggesting. As usual, he was commanding but in an oddly subdued fashion, so that Ellis had the impression she could have refused if she wanted to. This was so unusual that she was debating the point with herself when Vanno looked up from her everlasting knitting.

'You'd sleep better for it, Ellis,' she said frankly, reverting from Welsh to her 'Cheltenham Ladies' clipped English, a sure sign she was in a managerial mood. 'It'll walk off that meal, the best you've eaten since you arrived. Until now, you've been pecking like a bird.'

Ellis went on considering. She was in no mood for another confrontation with Gideon, she felt rather fragile; furthermore, recent experience had reinforced her opinion that it was unwise to take him at face value. He was crafty, two-faced, with a tongue like a serpent, and she didn't trust him as far as she could throw him.

'Davey might wake,' she demurred.

Vanno's dark eyes twinkled and her plain, rather gaunt face relaxed into a knowing smile. 'But I shall be here,' she pointed out. 'If he does, I'll go up and tell him a story. Although I don't think there's much chance of that, he's tired himself out. It's the first time ever I've seen him sit still. Go along, I dare say you have a lot to talk about.' She waved peremptorily. 'Take a coat, though, it's turned quite chilly.'

There was no escape; Ellis knew the futility of objecting or saying she was too tired. For some reason, her foster-mother was playing Cupid with all the finesse of a steamroller—some Cupid! Sixty-plus and knitting a sweater!—and there was a light of purpose in her eyes. Abruptly, Ellis gave in; she couldn't fight the two of them. Vanno was used to having her own way, she chaired dozens of local committees and had long learned how to get it. 'Be wilfully blind to everybody's opinion but your own', was her motto.

Reluctantly, Ellis changed her slippers for country-type lace-ups—she wasn't risking another tumble—and went to drag her sheepskin jacket from its peg in the hallway before following Gideon out into the darkness. He hadn't said anything yet, had he? She'd kill him if he had!

'Have you been hinting things behind my back?' She taxed him with it as soon as they were out of earshot of the house. 'Or, worse still, right under my nose? Was that what all the Welsh was about? I thought we were going to keep it quiet until the lodge was ready.'

'We are, and I haven't said a word about a wedding,' he stressed the word 'wedding' blandly but the arm about her slender waist was forceful as he steered her further away from the house and in the direction of the path upwards into the hills, to halt by the gate. 'I've only been preparing the ground. I hint better in Welsh,' he added.

'I know you, Gideon,' she accused acidly. 'You're up to something. You used to spoil things for me when I was a kid; a couple of words I didn't understand and it was Gwenny who went on an outing while I stayed at home with Vanno.'

'Less trouble that way.' He shrugged dismissively. 'Stop harking back to the past, Ellis. Vanno's putting one and one together and coming up with the right answer. I believe she's been doing it ever since you

wrote to say you and the boy were coming. Of course,'
he continued with an odd, fond amusement in his
voice, 'as the days go by, we'll have to give her something definite to ease her mind.'

'As the days go by?' Her ears had caught that softening and she could have wept that it was all for Vanno,
with nothing left over for herself. Coupled with her
nervousness and feelings of guilt, it made her feel like
an outcast so that she had interrupted him harshly. She
continued on the same abrasive note.

'You may start dropping hints when I think the time
is right, which will be when the lodge is ready and not
before. Even then, I'll need time to furnish it. On
second thoughts, you'd better leave it to me.'

'Giving orders already?' he reproved her mildly,
which sent her eyebrows into arches of suspicion and
disbelief. 'You sound like a shrew. But no,' the velvet
glove was discarded and the steel came through
strongly, battering at her bruised sensibilities. 'I shan't
leave it to you,' he continued firmly. 'You say you
know me, but I also know you, Ellis, and how quiet and
secretive you can be when you've something to hide.'

'A mind-reader,' she sneered. 'Or an amateur
psychologist.'

'Perhaps a bit of both, but whatever, you don't fool
me! You've loosened up a bit—you don't seem anywhere near as withdrawn as you used to be—but you
still hide too much. Iron-hard with yourself.' His voice
went lilting on, lulling her suspicions. 'And your face a
little mask to conceal what you're thinking. Gwenny
was all on the surface; smiles, tears, temper, it all
showed; but with you, nothing!'

'Who's harking back to the past now?' Ellis made herself serene. He had accused her of secrecy, but what was the use of trying to explain? There weren't any words she could put together to show him how it had been for her in those old days. The insecurity she had felt, the fear of being sent back to the Home if she did or said anything wrong. When she had at last begun to feel secure, it had been too late to change. Reticence had become an integral part of her, or perhaps that was just the way she was built.

The sound of Gideon's voice penetrated her musings, a voice which seemed again to have lost its aggressive timbre and she hurried to pay attention, praying she hadn't missed too much of what he was saying.

'. . . the time would never be right for you.' He was being benevolently autocratic and his arm was back around her waist, imprisoning her as if there were something unpleasant coming and he was going to make her face it. 'You seem to prefer the *fait accompli* situation, but surprise isn't good for old ladies. We don't want her flat on her back with shock when we make the announcement.'

'I've said I'll tell her and I will!' The new Ellis, the calm, capable woman of the world, with hardly a trace of the fearful child who hid every emotion, was on the verge of losing her temper again, she could feel it slipping away, but her mask was still in place and her voice, although definite, was quiet.

'It's my place to do the telling,' he retorted and started on his 'sly humour' thing again. 'You will stand at my side with your hand in mine and look suitably demure, even a little embarrassed at the speed of things. Trouble is,' he continued easily, 'Vanno's a shrewd one, even if she does tend to leap to the wrong conclusions.'

'What wrong conclusions?' she demanded roughly and drew in a sharp breath as he laughed. She didn't think she had ever heard him actually laugh before and it did queer things to her, made her go soft and mushy so that it was only with difficulty that she stopped her whole body from softening.

'As if you didn't know.' He was back to mockery. 'And it wasn't for me to disabuse her; I thought you would prefer her to keep her romantic illusions. Our motives, *cariad*,' he tut-tutted so blandly, she was now sure he was laughing at her. 'You surely don't want her to know I'm marrying you for your money; she wouldn't like that at all!'

There was now a little light. The moon had risen, but it was only low in the sky, partly hidden by the clouds rushing across its brightness. Ellis thought she heard the hoot of an owl as at last Gideon's arm relaxed its hold and she stood free. She raised her face and a fitful moonbeam lit it to a cold, detached purity.

'Romantic illusions?' She shook her head wearily; keeping up her end in this duel of words with Gideon was very exhausting, especially with him in what seemed a new mood. She had seen him cold, hard, arrogant, disapproving, she had felt his temper reaching out to chill her in its bitter rage, but never before had he behaved like this: easily, with a turn of almost puckish humour. It made her suspicious, and in the dim light of the moon she examined him closely from beneath lowered lids.

The cap of glossy curls clinging so closely to his well-shaped skull, his high forehead and the arched brows over slanting, faun-like eyes beneath heavy lids fringed with ridiculous, almost feminine lashes. A bold, hawklike nose and a mouth which promised heaven or hell; you paid your money and you took a chance. A satyr, perhaps, he had that wickedly malicious look about him, and involuntarily her eyes slid down over lean hips and long legs. She was half expecting to see neat, goat-like hooves, and she found herself blinking with surprise at perfectly normal feet laced into equally normal shoes.

Something moved in her stomach to release a warm flood which filled her with fright. Dear god, *no*! Not this way! It would be suicide, complete and irreversible, and she would never recover from it, no longer be a person in her own right. How could she feel like this when he wasn't even touching her! Love she both wanted and needed, but not this sort. This was the ultimate, it was chains, mental as well as physical. In her mind she could almost hear the metallic clink as link forged on link, and feel the weight of the iron binding her. But there was nothing she could do now; already it was too late. Hours, months, years too late.

'What exactly have you been saying?' she demanded crossly and as a little light began to burn in her mind, illuminating the dark corners where her fears hid like bats in the dark, 'Have you made Vanno think there might have been something between us before I went off to London? Oh, you couldn't have done that! I know I behaved like a starstruck idiot, but I was barely seventeen and very young for my age.'

'I didn't have to.' He was alarmingly cheerful so that she cringed and his next words came like a knell of doom. 'Vanno had that idea in mind already, *cariad*. I merely hinted that she might be right.'

Ellis now knew how a sheep felt when it was gently being chivvied through a gate. Everything very quiet and gentle; the silly beast must not be frightened. The hairs on the back of her neck rose in a prickle of warning.

'It just isn't true,' she wailed, 'you know it isn't! I had a teenage thing about you and you were cruel to be kind. I can see that now. I'm sure Vanno never thought anything bad. If she does now, it's because of some idea you've planted in her mind!' She controlled her face so that nothing showed, but her hands were clenched so tightly, the nails were biting into her palms.

'That's always possible! I may have said something she could have taken either way,' he admitted soothingly. 'Only a hint to set her mind at rest and pave the way.'

'You think of everything!' She ground her teeth. 'Even excuses!'

'Somebody has to.' He was back to blandness. 'She is a bit worried about you and Davey, she likes having you here; she thinks it's a better, healthier place to live and she doesn't like the idea of your returning to London with a child clinging to your skirts and no man to protect you from the wicked world. I've half hinted that I'll keep you here this time, and, unlike you, she has great faith in my powers of persuasion.'

'This time! Oh, you're so thoughtful!' Ellis shook her head while she pretended a syrupy admiration. Unfortunately, she couldn't keep up the pretence, it crumbled away into biting rhetoric. 'Just what have you said? Nothing to my credit, I'll be bound, and now, I suppose, Vanno thinks I'm a light-minded hussy.'

'She doesn't.' Gideon slid an arm round her waist

again, a spurious gesture of comfort, and although she cringed away from his touch with a dramatic shudder, he kept it there. 'She knows you're nothing of the kind. To her way of thinking, all the blame is mine for first seducing you when you were at in an impressionable age. No, don't hit me.' He caught her balled fist before it had travelled more than a few inches and continued blithely. 'I didn't say a word. But Vanno . . .' he shrugged. 'She understands human nature and I thought it better not to protest too much.'

'Seduced me!' Ellis squawked wrathfully and continued shrilly. 'You've let her think that? You insidious liar! Oh, hell!' She felt the slow, difficult tears smarting in her eyes. She refused to let them fall, instead she stood very still, fighting for control. She sniffed and took her courage in both hands. 'You're speaking as if it were true when it isn't! We never . . .'

'No, never,' he agreed blandly. 'But Vanno needed some answers and I had to hint at something she would believe.'

'You damn liar!' She spat out the words as though each one had a nasty taste. 'And she believed you! Oh, hell! I can understand that; you'll have *me* believing it if I stay here with you much longer!'

'We have until half past ten,' he said irritatingly with a suggestive leer. 'That's when she locks the door.'

CHAPTER SIX

'HOW dare you?' Ellis's breath caught as she felt a sweet hunger flooding through her and was tempted. Gideon had been renowned for never refusing, but she stamped on the impulse just in time and defined it clinically. Not love, nothing so gentle and beautiful; merely passion, a fierce need and nothing to be proud of. What she was now feeling was no more than a physical reaction common to widows. And did Gideon know about that? Of course he did, the rat! She drew in a deep breath of the cool night air and turned nasty.

'What a pity I can't remember.' She became biting. 'It must be more than seven years ago, too long to account for Davey but I'm so forgetful! Tell me, what was it like—was I good, or did you find me a bit of a disappointment?'

'Don't be crude,' he admonished. 'You were as shy and pure as the driven snow, but quite perfect.' His voice was filled with a lilting mockery as he embroidered the tale. 'And I was bereft when you told me our relationship must end, that you could never be content with the little I had to offer. You were leaving Dyffryn to carve out a career for yourself in the big city. But, having my memories to console me, I was happy for you to go and I further consoled myself with the thought of future visits to London.'

'And I've let you down by forgetting it!' Deliberately,

she let her voice slide into malicious mockery before she reverted to crispness. 'You've missed your profession, Gideon; you should have been on the stage.' She shook her head in pseudo-admiration before she allowed herself to think of the damage he might have done to the friendship and trust between her and her foster-mother.

Vanno's heart was big enough to take in a whole world of people and their weaknesses, but she was very straitlaced when it came to her own family. But, Ellis tried to comfort herself; she wasn't real family. Vanno would possibly forgive her a mythical false step, but it would be different if it were Gwenny! Once disappointed in her daughter, Vanno would be quite capable of the old 'Never darken my doors again' routine. At least, that was what Gwenny had said, and Gwenny should know!

'You didn't tell her all that!' Her voice grated on the protest as she felt her cold hands grow damp with nervous perspiration. Gideon was inventing a tale to his own advantage and she could hardly believe it, but she knew, from past experience, that he was bloody-minded enough to do anything if it suited him.

'I didn't really tell her anything.' He stood back from her and she caught the breath of his amusement. 'I didn't have to, she told me! I told you, she is very understanding.'

'So you encouraged her!' Ellis's voice was hoarse with suppressed rage. 'I might have known you'd stop at nothing. Your way of getting even with me, and damn you for doing it! You never wanted me here, you always hated me,' she accused wildly. 'You still do. You always blamed me for everything and you haven't changed a bit! Now you're fouling up me and Vanno, letting her think we . . . Well, this time you've overstepped the mark. Tomorrow, Davey and I go back to London and our deal's off!'

'No.' His hands dropped to her shoulders, holding her still. 'You can't do that, Ellis. Think of . . .'

'. . . Vanno?' she interrupted savagely. '*You* think of her!'

'Actually,' he said it maliciously, paying no heed to her temper or her wild accusations, 'I was thinking of your petrol tank. It's as dry as a bone,' the moonlight silvered his face to stone, 'and I'll see it stays that way. It was your idea that we marry; we made a bargain, and now I'm holding you to it. Life with you won't be a bed of roses, but it should be stimulating if your everchanging moods are anything to go by.'

'Then you can stay here and be stimulated all by yourself,' she squalled, but with a faint taste of triumph in her gut. Mission accomplished, all the loose ends tied up; and so easily, could there be a catch in it? The triumph died in a welter of doubt and she was left with the old, aching sorrow.

'I'm going back to the house,' she announced breathily. 'I shall make myself a cup of tea and go to bed. In the morning, when I wake, everything will be back to normal and I shall know I've dreamed it all!'

'Good girl,' he complimented her without a shred of remorse. 'Make it tea for two. Your trouble, *cariad*, is that you haven't an eye for detail, and forcing you to see sense has given me a thirst!'

Ellis made her tea, one tea-bag in a mug—let Gideon make his own if he wanted it that badly—with enough milk so that she could gulp it down quickly and hustle herself upstairs before he came in. Sleep didn't come quickly, she thought of Robert instead. She closed her eyes and fancied she heard his voice, acerbic at times but always encouraging. But behind her eyelids, it was Gideon's face she saw. Restless, she put her gloomy thoughts to one side and sought the rather bitter humour of her situation.

Here she was, scheming for a place for Davey and on the verge of success. It would be sheer stupidity to give up now when she was so close, closer than she had ever expected to be and in so little time. She'd not had a real plan, only a dream that somehow she could establish Davey here, where he belonged. She had not expected to be able to do that quickly but the opportunity had come and she had taken it. She had grasped the nettle boldly, but if you did that, it wasn't supposed to sting this badly. In the darkness, she stifled a bitter laugh in her pillow. Fate played the damnedest tricks!

No story she could ever have thought of would have been so convenient as the one Gideon had invented to embarrass her and force her hand. Now, she could keep the promise she had made to herself and Vanno could keep her illusion. Superstitiously, she crossed her fingers; things could still go wrong and the price she was paying was high; it was going to cost her so much more than money!

On the edge of sleep, her eyes flew open and she stared into the darkness, wishing she knew exactly what Gideon had hinted to Vanno. It would be so much more convincing if they both told the same story. As it stood now, she would have to play it by ear if Vanno questioned her, but then again, Vanno wasn't the type of ask personal questions. With a weary sigh, she gave up and closed her eyes, resolving to let Gideon do any other explaining; his serpent-type brain would slither through anything.

In the morning, Vanno had laid the breakfast table for three and Ellis felt a sharp stab of disappointment. Something must have shown on her face, for her foster-mother at once became consoling, but briskly, which ruined the effect.

'Only gone for the day, *cariad;* he'll be back late after-noon. Didn't he tell you?'

'Probably,' Ellis shrugged. 'And equally probably, I wasn't listening at the time. Davey, you know. he chatters nonstop and I have to keep my eye on him perpetually, he's not used to so much freedom.'

Vanno nodded understandingly as she slid eggs and bacon on to plates and put them in the warming oven. 'And he said to tell you the builder has started repairing the roof of the lodge and you're to go down there and tell him what alterations you want.'

'Quick work!' Ellis seated Davey at the table and poured milk over his cornflakes.

'Not that quick.' Vanno seated herself and commenced her usual breakfast of tea and thinly cut, well-buttered toast. 'I believe Gideon made the arrangements some time ago. It was let, you know, but the tenants left; they were quite old and how they managed without a proper bathroom, I'll never know. They went to live with a married daughter in the Potteries. Gideon had the idea of living down there himself but that was before he knew it was to come to you. Anyway,' she gave Ellis an uncomplicated smile of pleasure which made her cringe, 'it'll be a nice walk for you and Davey; a long way, but it's going to be a fine day and you can take your time about it.'

'Aren't you coming? I might need some advice.' Ellis, who had never felt any lack of company as long as she was with Davey, suddenly felt lonely.

'I'd have liked nothing better.' Vanno shook her head regretfully. 'But I've a meeting of the school governors at eleven. We're interviewing for a new assistant head and there's a taxi coming for me at half past ten. Just look at the clock, I shall have to hurry, if I'm not to keep the man waiting. You have a quiet morning, Ellis; go down to the lodge this afternoon. There's a beef casserole in the oven for your lunch, save you cooking.'

'You'd like that, Davey?' Ellis had to wait for a reply, Davey's mouth was full of cornflakes and he was crunching like mad.

'See my dog first,' he piped hopefully. 'Could we take him for a walk?

'He's only five weeks old.' Ellis put everything else out of her mind to concentrate on sweet reason. 'He couldn't walk that far and he still needs his mother.'

'I could keep him warm in my anorak.' Davey looked at her soulfully and for a second, the indefinable resemblance to Gideon was there on his face. Ellis caught her breath and stooped over him so that Vanno's eyes shouldn't see it, but the likeness vanished as quickly as it had come and she let out the air in her lungs with a gasp.

'No.' She was firm. 'He'd smell all wrong when you take him back to the "hen", and maybe his mother would think he didn't belong to her any more and refuse to feed him. You can't have him until Gideon says you may.'

Davey disdained a ride in his pushchair down to the lodge. He wasn't a baby any more, he was big, so Ellis let him push it. His bright chatter should have enlivened the walk, but nearly every word which fell from his infant lips deepened her gloom.

'Gideon says I'm big enough to ride, Ellis. He says he knows a pony who'll like me and we won't never go back to London and Idris says he'll be my friend when I'm bigger and I can sit with him on the bus when we go to school.' Ellis listened with one ear while she eyed her car malevolently as they walked past it. After years of living in London she had lost the habit of walking, and although her crêpe-soled flatties were comfortable, the mile-long walk up to the Plas seemed to stretch in front of her endlessly. By the time they reached the *'hen'*, she was only too glad to sink on to a bale of straw and indulge in some wishful thinking—for a big, red London bus!

'He's growing, he's twice as big as yesterday.' Davey brought her the squirming pup to inspect, his hands gentle about the warm little body. 'We *can* stay here, Ellis, can't we, so's I can have a pony?' And Ellis, for whom the die was cast, could only nod weakly.

It was an even longer walk from the Plas to the lodge but all downhill so that Davey took it in his stride. He allowed her to push the pushchair while he skipped merrily ahead of her along what had once been a well-used road but now was little better than a cart-track. He kept up a constant barrage of embarrassing questions, all prefaced with 'Gideon says' and ending with 'I can, can't I, Ellis?' so that by the time they arrived at their destination, she discovered she had promised him everything he had asked for, except her permission to swim in the river with Idris.

Outwardly, the lodge looked to be in good condition and the local builder—a man she had known since she was a child—was encouraging, even when she had to skip aside to dodge a shower of slates which his men were dislodging from the roof.

'Not to worry about a few broken slates, Ellis; it's what's under them that counts, and the timbering's as good as the day it was put up. Well-built, you see; oak and mahogany and good red brick, all solid stuff. It's not bad at all, considering how long it's been empty, must be all of four years,' was his verdict. 'Mind you, the rooms aren't as big as you'd find in a modern house, but I've thought of a way to get round that.'

As Ellis watched a bright-eyed Davey exploring the overgrown wilderness of the garden, she also managed to listen attentively to the builder as he rearranged the house in his mind and listed a few improvements. He recommended a wide archway instead of a door between the kitchen and a small parlour so that she could use the latter as a walk-through dining-area, and another two small rooms could be opened out into one to make a reasonable-sized louge. There was already a downstairs washroom and toilet which only needed bringing up to date with a new suite; the smallest of the four bedrooms would convert nicely to a bathroom and a shower could be installed in an otherwise useless box-room.

She pictured the house as it was all described graphically and finally nodded in content. It would be a good place to live in, and the repairs and alterations would take less than a month. Now that she was committed, she wanted the waiting-time reduced as much as possible so that she could walk into her own home. The house in London had never seemed to be really hers; she had always felt more like a caretaker. She would ask Martin to dispose of it and the contents and she would start again from scratch. A new beginning, a new life.

Ellis arrived back at her foster-mother's house weary and overheated. Davey, who had skipped, run and hopped all the way down to the lodge, had fallen asleep at just the wrong moment so that she'd had to put him in the pushchair and push him back, uphill all the way, and the sight of the Land Rover standing in the lane didn't improve her temper. Her hair had come loose so that it hung in tangles about her shoulders, the collar of her silk shirt was damp with perspiration and she had snagged her skirt. She prayed that Vanno had returned; she didn't feel in the mood to cope with Gideon's two-edged remarks all by herself.

Gideon looked up from the pot of tea he was brewing, frowned at her dishevelled appearance and removed the sleeping child from her arms.

'She's not back yet.' He caught her wandering glance and held it. 'Always the same with these eleven o'clock meetings; no time to get much done before lunch so they drag on. Where shall I put him?'

'On the couch in the parlour,' she told him moodily, 'and while you're at it, say a prayer he won't sleep too long or we'll not get him to bed before midnight.'

'Snappish,' he murmured when he returned and eyed her dishevelled state. 'You look and sound like an ill-tempered wife; and after a lovely afternoon in the fresh air. Have a cup of tea, it might sweeten your temper.'

'There's nothing wrong with my temper,' she said. 'I'm tired, that's all. You try pushing Davey uphill for several miles, you'd be tired as well! Please, Gideon, get me some petrol for my car.'

'If you promise not to run out on me.'

'I promise,' she sighed wearily. 'Will Vanno be home soon?'

'You're joking!' He eyed her sardonically. 'They're interviewing and there are three candidates. Vanno won't be back before seven, which gives us time for discussion. Three weeks on Saturday, will that suit you?'

'No!' Ellis didn't pretend not to know what he was talking about. 'Too soon, the lodge won't be ready.'

'It will.' Gideon gave her a tight smile. 'In five weeks. Vanno will look after Davey while we're away on honeymoon.'

'No, no honeymoon.' Ellis was decisive. 'This is a business arrangement.'

'Of course,' he agreed with a wry twist to his mouth. It was a beautiful mouth, Ellis thought, and indulged in a wild daydream that it would be tender, that his whole face would soften and his dark eyes would glow instead of glinting. She looked away, making pictures in her mind, and shivered before she banished them to return to reality to try to catch up on what he was saying.

'. . . this isn't London, we're known here and if we don't want raised eyebrows, we'll have to put on some sort of a show. That's settled then, three weeks next Saturday. Can you still blush, Ellis?'

'What do you think?' She eyed him malevolently. 'Did I ever?'

'Not that I recall.' He shook his head. 'I used to think

you might be frail; lily-pale always, you didn't even get a tan in the summer. Church or the register office, and are you going to tell Davey or shall I?'

'I'll give it some thought.' She gave him a withering glance; being curt was the only way she could handle it without making an idiot of herself. She became busy collecting a cup and saucer from the dresser but he set her aside, quite gently, pushing her into Vanno's big Windsor rocker, pouring her a cup of tea and fetching her slippers from where she had left them in the scullery.

'Be still.' He stooped to unlace her shoes and she stared down at the top of his dark head bemusedly. She wanted to push her fingers through his curls, straighten them out and sweep them off his high forehead; instead, she locked her fingers together so tightly her knuckles were white. His hands were cool and competent but his touch was doing devastating things to her heartbeat and breathing, and when the telephone shrilled to distract him, she didn't know whether to be glad or sorry as he rose to answer it.

'I'll be down there straight away,' was all he said before he slammed the phone down. 'Vanno's been hurt.' He turned to her, all his gentleness gone. 'She's in the cottage hospital at Machy.'

'Oh, no.' Ellis nearly moaned it as her heart gave an almighty thump and started to beat fast. 'Is she . . . is it . . .?' Hastily, she slid her feet back into her shoes, tying the laces all anyhow. 'I'll come with you.'

'You'd better stay here. What about Davey?'

'He may have woken, he usually does in the daytime if there's a noise.' Her voice came muffled from the folds of the sweater she was pulling over her head.

As her mouth emerged from the turtle neck, she went on calmly, 'If not, I'll have him on my lap. Pity my car's dry,' she added venomously. 'It would have been quicker than the Land Rover.'

Ellis held a sleeping Davey in her arm and tried one-handedly to pin up her bedraggled hair while the Land Rover bumped and groaned down the narrow road. It was better when they turned on to the main road from Dyffryn to the coast, Gideon put his foot down and the old vehicle roared its appreciation as it thundered along. Ellis, with a mouthful of hairpins, was perforce silent and Gideon—she stole a glance at him—was looking worried. The bond between him and his aunt was very strong, one didn't need to be a mind-reader to know that. Vanno had been a second mother to him when his own mother had died.

She tried to identify her own worry, but somehow it wasn't there any longer, and although she half distrusted this calm feeling, she was quite certain that everything would be all right. The way she was now was not a bit as she had been the night Robert was killed. That night, she'd heard the fog warning on the late news and a premonition had made her cold all over. There had been no rest for her and she had sat up all night until the phone rang just after dawn. However, she knew it would be useless to attempt to comfort Gideon by quoting a 'feeling'; he would either laugh in her face or condemn her as a superstitious freak.

He didn't ease the vehicle up until Machy's Victorian Gothic clocktower came into view and Ellis was surprised to see it was only six o'clock; they seemed to have taken hours to get here. Obligingly, Davey woke as they drew up in the hospital car park, but it was quite safe to leave him; Llew, like a black and white shadow, had jumped into the driver's seat as Gideon vacated it. He wouldn't allow anybody to enter the car and neither would he allow Davey to get out of it. To him, who could herd a whole flock of sheep from point A to point B without a single mishap, one small boy was a minor task!

Nevertheless, Ellis played safe and, after strapping Davey securely in the front passenger seat, she gave him a stern warning not to wriggle free, together with the car manual out of the glove compartment plus a felt-tipped pen from her bag. They would keep him occupied while she and Gideon were in the hospital, and if he ruined the manual, it wouldn't matter. It was at least ten years old and Gideon ought to know it off by heart. If he didn't, so much the worse for him!

The doctor had waited for them but he concentrated on Gideon while Ellis found herself fobbed off with the ward sister, a very efficient lady who offered Ellis tea and sympathy in her office since the patient was only permitted one visitor. Doctor's orders!

'From what I gather, everything happened in a moment.' The ward sister spread her hands with a crackle of starch and a mystified wag of her head which nearly unseated her old-fashioned cap—starched and gophered muslin frills with a bow under her chin. 'There were several eye-witnesses but not a single coherent tale between them. Mrs Rhys-Williams was walking along the pavement when suddenly she was in the road, right in front of a car coming towards her. Luckily, it was only crawling up to the junction, the lights were against it.'

For a second, Ellis had been thrown off balance. 'Mrs Rhys-Williams' had such an unfamiliar ring to her, who had never called that lady anything but Aunt Vanno and later plain Vanno. She took that second to adjust and then nodded.

'Is she badly . . .' but she was given no chance to complete the question, starched and frilled authority was in command.

'Nothing broken, although unfortunately she can't seem to remember what happened. There's some extensive bruising which will be painful, and shock, of course, which at her age could be serious. The doctor wishes to keep her in for a day or so to make sure there are no side effects.'

'You'll have difficulty.' Ellis spoke almost without thinking and the sister lost some of her stiffness.

'Don't I know that already!' Starch crackled again as she gave a restrained chuckle. 'She and I are quite well acquainted, Mrs Blake; we're both on the Welfare Committee. I'm sorry you can't see her now but orders are orders; the doctor said just the one visitor. Besides, she's been sedated, soon she'll be asleep—the best thing for her in her present condition—but when she comes round properly . . .'

'She'll run the hospital for you!' Everything was going to be all right and the last little bit of tension seeped away, leaving Ellis feeling confident enough to smile, and her smile was infectious. It gained her a cup of tea, a shortbread biscuit and a quick peep at a somnolent Vanno, over whom the doctor and Gideon were hovering protectively.

'It's a hospital!' Davey had watched her approach to the car and when she opened the door, his small face was pinched with fright. 'Are you sick, Ellis?'

'No,' she soothed, 'Aunty Vanno's had an accident crossing the road, the doctor and the nurses are making her better. She'll be coming home soon.'

'Tomorrow or the next day?' Davey was hopeful. 'Like when I had my tonsils out. I'll pick some flowers for her for when she comes home.' He contemplated the situation and arrived at what was to him an inescapable conclusion. 'There ought to be a lollipop lady, Ellis. You make them get one.'

Gideon's return to the Land Rover stopped any further conversation. It was heralded by Llew slinking into the back, leaving a film of black hair all over the driver's seat, but Gideon either didn't notice or didn't care. He restored Davey to the rear seat and strapped him in without a word and his face was set in such tight lines, Ellis thought better of the insouciant remark hovering on the end of her tongue. Instead, she touched his arm and was rewarded by a lessening of the tightness.

'No serious damage, nothing broken,' he murmured, too low for Davey to hear. 'She says she doesn't remember a thing! They're going to keep her in as long as possible. The doctor wants to run some tests.'

'She won't stay, not unless they tie her down to the bed.' Ellis filled in the gap left by his silence, but wasn't a bit surprised when he started on the 'angry' thing. It was probably a cover-up for his worry.

'What on earth made her trot off into the road like that?' he growled savagely. 'It's utterly unlike her.'

'Something in a shop window.' Ellis shrugged. 'Somebody she wanted to speak to, or maybe she just stumbled off the pavement. You asked her?'

'No sense to be got from her, too full of dope,' he rasped, 'and only worried about you having to do the cooking!'

'Probably more worried about you having to eat the results.' Ellis tried a comforting noise; it was no use both of them being uptight. 'Let's go home,' she suggested, 'I shall personally burn you a couple of steaks for dinner.'

Later that night, Ellis woke from an uneasy sleep with the feeling that something was different. Her first thought was for Davey, and it was only when she heard his steady breathing that she allowed herself to think backwards. The steaks hadn't been burned; they had been a bit rare but not too much so, and the barbecue sauce had been a masterpiece. Even her stir-fried vegetables—a packet from the freezer and done in the stainless steel, round-bottomed mixing bowl because Vanno didn't possess a wok—had been successful in a soggy kind of way. There had been no complaints, but on the other hand there had been no compliments, even though Llew had dined exclusively on tinned dog food and biscuit because there were no leftovers.

So, it couldn't be the food which had wakened her at this extraordinary hour. Maybe her restlessness was caused by some subconscious worry about Vanno, although a suspicion lingered that she had been a bit heavy-handed with the spices for the sauce. There had to be something to account for her waking up. With a groan for a disturbed night—broken sleep always made her irritable—she looked at her watch. The fingers registered nearly two a.m. and the house was as silent as a tomb.

Again, she looked at her watch while her sleep-drugged mind coped with the problem of how she could see the time so clearly at two a.m. in the dark, and on a watch which was more dressy than utilitarian. At last she identified the reason. The kitchen light was still on, it was shining out through the uncurtained kitchen window and the reflected glow of it lit up the bedroom. Vanno didn't like lights left on and, dragging her dressing-gown about her to cover her nightdress, Ellis pattered barefoot down the stairs to switch it off.

But the light was on for a reason. Gideon hadn't yet gone to bed, he was sitting in Vanno's rocker, fully dressed except for his jacket and staring moodily at nothing. Quiet as she had been, he seemed to sense her presence and he turned his head to her wearily.

'Go back to bed, Ellis.' It was an order, uncompromising and bleak, but one she didn't fancy obeying.

'You need sleep as well, Gideon,' she retorted composedly, 'or you'll be snarling all over the breakfast table. Go to bed yourself. If you're waiting for a phone call from the hospital, I'll take it and wake you immediately.'

Gideon didn't reply to that, instead he surveyed her from head to foot and went off at a tangent. 'You shouldn't be walking barefoot on quarry tiles, Ellis. You'll get pneumonia.'

'Vanno says so!' she parroted and shook her head, wondering if it wouldn't be better to make him lose his temper; at least that would be a positive reaction. 'Look,' she demanded, and her tartness drew his attention so that his heavy eyelids rose and his dark eyes focused on her face after giving the rest of her a thorough going-over. She suffered it stolidly, refusing to show any trace of the little prickle of excited fear which ran down her spine, although her fingers clutched automatically at the edges of her dressing-gown, drawing them more closely together.

'What good do you think you're doing,' she continued crossly, 'sitting here glooming about something over which you have no control? For Pete's sake, go to bed and get some sleep. You may be needed in the morning.'

She watched as his hand closed on a fold of her dressing-gown and began pulling her towards him. She hunted for some resistance but somehow it was all gone; the tiredness and worry graven deep in his face had killed it, and when he had pulled her close enough, she put her arms about his shoulders and drew his head against her. She despised her weakness, she would have killed it if she could, but she could no longer help herself.

CHAPTER SEVEN

FOR what seemed a long time, Ellis stood there, holding his head against her breast, as she held Davey when he hurt himself or was frightened about something. She crooned comfortingly, as she would have done to Davey. 'Everything will be all right in the morning, you'll see,' she heard herself murmuring. 'Go to bed now and get some sleep. I'll wait up.'

She was washed clean of everything but pity and a wish to comfort and heal, and exactly when that pity turned into desire she didn't know. But he knew and she felt a wild response crackling between them as his arms tightened about her and his head nuzzled closer against her breast.

'Come with me, Ellis.' His softly voiced suggestion had seductive overtones, and when he lifted his head their eyes met and held for a long moment. Under his steady gaze, she could feel her heartbeat increase and a little ragged sigh escaped her lips. Why not accept? Why cry for the moon when she could never have it? Gideon wasn't offering her false coin, he wasn't pretending to a love he didn't feel. He was only asking for comfort, something to take her mind away from his worry about Vanno.

And it would be so easy to do as he'd suggested, they both needed it, but—her mind ran forward and stopped on doubt—was this the best she could hope for? *Would* everything be all right in the morning? He was a proud man, and already she had tied him to her with the heavy chain of her money to save the Plas. Wasn't that enough for him to clank around in? She fought back tears and became crisp.

'Why do I feel that's rather a grudging invitation?' she asked tartly, while her eyes noted the grey look of worry on his face and the dark shadow of stubble about his chin. 'Although I admit it's one I might have been tempted to accept at any other time,' she continued lightly, because lightly does it and this was not the moment to be heavy-handed. 'But just at the present, I don't think I'm in the mood to be used as a soporific for your tender conscience.'

'I don't have a tender conscience, you know that!' She had succeeded in pricking him out of his gloom and he was at last showing some signs of life and his famous temper. With a low growl which was almost a snarl, he quitted the rocking-chair with such force that the poor old thing nearly capsized backwards. Towering over her, he grabbed at her wrist and glared down at her, the nostrils of his high-bridged nose thinned with temper, 'I was merely issuing an invitation.'

'In which I'm not interested.' Ellis lied magnificently and went on to improve on her performance, gilding the lily with a vengeance. 'Vanno will be back soon, I'm sure of that, and how could I look her in the eye if I'd been abusing her hospitality by romping with you in the spare bedroom while her back was turned?' She let her mouth curve into a very small but bitter smile. 'Perfect I may not be, but I draw the line at some things. Meanwhile, if you're that desper-

ate, I'm sure you have a friend who would accommo-
date you in an emergency, so leap into your trusty
chariot and go find her. But, please, do have a shave
first. You look like something the cat's dragged in!'

For a moment, the expression on his face was so
fierce she thought she was going to be slapped, but
suddenly he relaxed and she watched his features
dissolve into pure mockery.

'Am I going to have a broad-minded wife?' His
eyebrows rose satanically and his heavy-lidded eyes
narrowed to gleaming slits.

'Oh, absolutely,' she assured him caustically before
she tortured her features into angelic innocence. 'I'm
noted for my broad-mindedness and my sweet, forgiving nature.'

'I knew it,' he growled venomously. 'The original
plaster saint.'

Ellis maintained her calm. She stared down at his
hand, still fastened on her wrist, and kept her eyes
there until the clasp loosened and she stood free. If
her little laugh was a trifle forced, he didn't seem to
notice.

'That's the image I project,' she murmured. 'And I
intend to keep it that way. We mustn't shatter the
plaster; who knows what might crawl out of the
cracks.'

She achieved the effect she was aiming for. Gideon
stormed out of the kitchen—the only thing he didn't
do was slam the door—and up the stairs to his own
room with little regard for Davey's slumbers, and
when he had gone she sank into the rocker, drawing
one of Vanno's knitted shawls about her trembling
body and feeling vaguely comforted by the warmth

he'd left on the cushions. Hearts did not break, she told herself; they only got bruised and ached a bit as hers was aching now. Virtue was its own reward but—her lips twisted wryly—she wasn't feeling virtuous or rewarded, anything but; so she ached.

It would have been so easy to go with him wherever he wanted, give him whatever he wanted, but she wouldn't bind him to her in that way. So, she had only herself to blame for the frustration which filled her. For one mad moment she contemplated going back to bed, but she knew if she did that she'd probably choose the wrong door, accidentally-on-purpose. She would walk in on Gideon and he, damn him, would probably be waiting for her because he'd known she wanted him. And once he had cooled down, this was what he would be expecting her to do.

Vanno's noisy cistern gurgled audibly and Ellis's eyes glittered with a fiendish satisfaction. Gideon was using the hot tap—not taking a shower, Vanno didn't have one—he was probably shaving in expectation of what was to come. Let him, she was going to stay right where she was, she wouldn't be tempted; not even if he had a chin as smooth as a baby's bottom. And with a sigh, half regret and half self-mockery, she curled up in the rocker, numb with weariness, and commenced her self-imposed vigil.

She woke to morning light, a heavenly aroma of bacon and coffee and the soft splutter of frying eggs, and she blinked at her surroundings sleepily. Some time during the night, while she'd slept, she had been moved from the rocker to lie, covered with a blanket and one of Vanno's knitted woolly covers, on the old-fashioned settle beneath the window. Davey was dressed and crunching cornflakes at the table, and he hailed her opened eyes with a wave of his spoon which sent milk and flakes flying.

'Aunty Vanno's better,' he announced importantly. 'She's had her breakfus and Gideon says you aren't a good watchdog, he says you went to sleep on duty. We're going to see her s'afternoon. I washed myself and Gideon dressed me but I had to show him how to button me up.'

'Breakfast, Ellis?' Gideon looked at her from where he was tending the frying-pan, and there was something about that look which made her aware of her dishevelled state, a glint in his dark eyes and a small smile about his mouth which was so intimate that it almost made her get up and run away. She conquered the desire by yawning, staying where she was and demanding a cup of coffee.

'You're looking better this morning.' She said it as their fingers touched when he handed her the cup and saucer. 'See what continence does for you! You slept well?'

'Wass continens?' Davey picked up the new word and spoke with his mouth full.

'Big lumps of land; you'll learn about them later in school when you do geography.' Ellis said it swiftly to cover an awkward pause.

'Oh.' Davey sounded disappointed as he returned to his crunching. 'I thought it was pills to make Gideon sleep. Red ones, like Aunty Vanno has.' That made Ellis prick up her ears; she hadn't ever seen Vanno taking any sort of medication, but her foster-mother would have hidden that from her. However,

Davey's sharp eyes rarely missed anything he wasn't supposed to see. On the other hand, this was no time to ponder. Gideon was speaking and Davey had stopped listening; he was spooning up cornflakes like a madman with an eye fixed firmly on the frying-pan. He liked his bacon crisp but not crackly.

'It didn't make me sleep.' The corner of Gideon's mouth twitched. 'I stayed awake for a long time, thinking. I expect you did the same, Ellis. You look as though you did. Such self-discipline,' he added softly. 'I'll have to think of some way to overcome it. There wasn't any need for you suffer so.'

'Who says I suffered?' Ellis felt herself relaxing, she even heard herself chuckle. She sipped at her coffee and made a face. 'Drat you, Gideon, you've sugared it, I'll get fat!'

'I like 'em that way,'

'Plural "them"?' she arched an eyebrow and wrinkled her nose at him to cover her surprise. They were actually talking, and in a friendly way, almost bantering. She could hardly believe it. Gideon being friendly, and to *her*! Of course, it wouldn't last; he'd be back to suspicion and nastiness in no time.

'Singular,' he came back at her quickly, 'and a very confusing little lady at times,' he added significantly, and she thought that since he had unbent this far, she would meet him half-way. Some time or another, they would have to establish a working-relationship. While the going was good, she would take advantage of it.

'Something bothering you?' She raised an enquiring eyebrow. 'It's all in the mind—your mind,' she murmured mysteriously.

'So I've suspected for several days,' he answered

with an equal amount of mystery. 'Now, I'm quite certain. Do I apologise?'

Ellis drained her coffee before she looked up at him candidly. 'Better not,' she said quietly. 'Apologies rarely help. It might be wise to talk it out but not now.' She slid a glance to where Davey was industriously scraping the bottom of his cereal bowl. 'Little pitchers have big ears and there's one mind which is already sufficiently confused with the continens. We'll wait for a more opportune moment.'

'A good idea, but unfortunately not this morning.' He looked at her obliquely and she thought she detected a trace of regret in his eyes. 'There's a flock of sheep to be brought in for shearing,' he continued, 'You know how it is, Ellis; the work has to come first and then I've to be back to take you and Davey down to Machy this afternoon. We might have to quell a riot in the hospital. You understand?'

'Perfectly,' she nodded, well content. Gideon had explained something to her at last, even if it was only a sketchy plan of his morning's work. It was a step in the right direction, a compliment in its way, and he had never handed out many of those, not to her, so the opportune moment could wait a bit longer. She had the odd feeling that something good was on the way, something good enough to be worth waiting for.

After lunch, Ellis changed into a fresh shirt and skirt and Gideon drove them down to the hospital where Vanno would only admit to being a bit sore. Otherwise, she insisted there was nothing wrong with her, so why was everybody so bothered about an old woman who had taken a tumble?

'I had worse before Christmas when I fell down the

stairs,' she snorted. 'I don't know what they're making all the fuss about.'

'Because you don't remember how it happened,' Ellis said patiently. 'Were you this muddled when you fell down the stairs?' She sneaked the question in swiftly and watched as her foster-mother's face adopted a fleeting expression of confusion, hastily replaced by one of militancy.

'I shall remember,' she snapped, ignoring Ellis's question as though it had never been asked, 'as soon as people stop bothering me with questions. Give me some peace in my own home and a good night's sleep in my own bed—this one's like concrete—and it will all come back to me. I'm more concerned about my hat! I liked that hat and now it's ruined. I shall come home tomorrow,' she added with a challenging look at a hovering nurse.

'Has anything like this happened before?' Ellis asked Gideon as they were driving back to Dyffryn. 'What I mean is, has Vanno been falling about a lot? She mentioned an accident on the stairs.'

'Do you honestly think she'd tell me, even if she had?' Gideon snorted his disgust and Ellis thought about it.

'No,' she decided at last, 'she wouldn't have told anybody. She'd have pretended so hard it hadn't happened that she'd have convinced herself. But now I know how things are, I'll keep my eye on her in future. You talked to the doctor, what did he say?'

'Age, a heart murmur, high blood-pressure plus doing too much. She won't lead a quiet life, she's always rushing off to some damn committee and she doesn't take her medicine regularly. What's worse, as you said, she won't tell anybody. This is the first I've heard of it, yet apparently she's had the condition for quite some time.' Gideon snarled it, but Ellis paid no attention to the snarl; she merely nodded.

'Typically Vanno: pretend it isn't there and it'll go away. But this time she won't get away with it. She'll have medication for the blood-pressure and a diet sheet,' she said with a bland firmness. 'I'll see she sticks to both, and you, Gideon, can set yourself to eliminating half the committee meetings on her schedule.'

But it wasn't until a week later that Gideon brought Vanno home, seven long days and nights during which Gideon had been on his best behaviour and Ellis, free for the first time of his niggling little comments, flowered. He no longer treated her with suspicion—well, not very much—which was a step in the right direction. Neither did he go into his seduction routine, which was a relief. A woman, any woman she decided, was capable of standing just so much, and Ellis had reached her limit the night of Vanno's accident. Any further assault on her feelings and she would probably dissolve into a puddle of passion.

Instead, he was kind, thoughtful and very correct. He treated her like a piece of delicate china marked 'Fragile' and 'Do Not Drop'; he even put a couple of gallons of petrol in her car, although why she couldn't imagine; he drove her anywhere she wished to go in the Land Rover. But she liked to think it showed he was trusting her at last, and she began to feel hopeful, if a bit frustrated. Maybe life with him would be more than just tolerable; she might even be happy.

Meanwhile, she kept herself busy, getting into the routine of cleaning and cooking with evening visits to the hospital and afternoon trips down to the lodge where she and the builder put their heads together and discussed the possibilities of tacking a granny flat on the western end of the house. Space was no problem, the garden was far too big; the only difficulty would be in getting Vanno to come and live in it.

The instructions which came home with Vanno and her bottle of pills were explicit, and her low-fat diet sheet was mind-bending. Also she was to take only gentle exercise and rest as much as possible. That for a laugh! Vanno spent exactly one hour in her rocker before grabbing back the reins of household management, but in such a fumbling and haphazard way that Ellis suspected she had been frightened more badly than she had been hurt.

Luckily, a letter from the charity interested in Plas Dyffryn arrived the following morning, suggesting a meeting between principals later in the week, if convenient, and that gave Vanno something beside a butterless, pill-popping life to think about. Gideon read it out over the breakfast table, and his aunt in her usual benevolently bossy way began making arrangements.

'Porthmadog, isn't it? Friday would be convenient, I'll be feeling much better by then. Nothing may come of it, Gideon; well, it needn't if you don't want it to.' She turned a martial eye on her nephew. 'Just going to a meeting with the governors won't commit you to anything, and the change will be just what I need. A quiet day away from the house and if there's time and it's fine, we'll take Davey to Black Rock sands, and on the way back we can call in at Port Meirion, they've got a marvellous pottery shop there. I might treat myself if I see something I like.'

'You call that a quiet day?' Ellis snorted with laughter, but her protest was only a formality. Vanno's plans sounded a bit strenuous, but Gideon would see his aunt didn't overtire herself. His swift, dark glance and a very slight inclination of his head told Ellis that, and she wondered whether she could opt out of the trip. She needed some solitude to plan ahead, and she didn't seem able to do that with Gideon perpetually hovering.

Out of the corner of her eye, she studied him again. No moonlight this time to give her fanciful ideas, only the morning sun to colour the details of an everyday picture. His height; his dark hair dampened and slicked to smoothness, but soon it would dry and curl; wide shoulders tapering down to slim hips, the absurd length of his eyelashes, his strong mouth with its rather sensual curve . . .

Why did she love this man? Over the years, he had given her little cause. Her quiet little love for Robert had been completely different, a warm friendliness, a gentle caring, undemanding, but so very safe and sure. With Gideon, she was sure of nothing; maybe she would be happy, maybe not, but it was a chance she had to take.

Loving a man made a woman weak, but as long as she hid it, Ellis could feel safe, although hiding it was a strain. Over the last two weeks, it had stretched her until she felt paper-thin and liable to tear at any moment. What she needed was a reason to duck out of this outing, but it would have to be a very good reason. Vanno wouldn't be satisfied with any old excuse.

Her chance arrived in the postman's bag, a conveniently delivered letter from Martin himself which Gideon dropped beside her plate on the morning of their departure for Porthmadog. She slit it open, read its innocuous contents—it was merely Martin being solicitous about the state of her health and her bank balance—and she tortured her forehead into a deep frown.

'You'll have to count me out,' she managed to sound bereft. 'A business phone call today, I shall have to be here to take it, but don't let that spoil things for you.' Out of the corner of her eye she noted the disappointment in Davey's quivering lip— he adored riding around in cars—and continued lightly. 'Davey's been looking forward to it,' she hesitated fractionally, 'and it would be a shame to make him miss it. Do you think you could manage him between you? He'll be no trouble.'

'Don't I know it! We'll have a splendid day, won't we, Davey?' Vanno was ecstatic at the prospect of having the child all to herself for a whole day, and the boy's definite nod followed by a beaming smile caused Ellis to catch her breath. Nothing was permanent, not even Davey. Already he was growing more independent, and she felt as though she was losing a small part of him. As time went by, she would lose more and more, but she had to learn to get used to that. She'd decided long ago not to be a possessive parent; that way, she could lose him for ever.

As the Land Rover turned out of the lane, she gave it a final wave and went back into the house which, silent, seemed to close around her, and around her waiting in it, equally silent. She fancied it was trying to tell her something, perhaps to be busy, that there was enough to do in the kitchen alone to satisfy a workaholic; but she ignored it, only clearing the breakfast dishes from the table and stacking them in the sink before going upstairs to make the beds and flick a duster round the bedrooms.

But Gideon's bedroom did peculiar things to her psyche. It smelled of male and she felt vaguely threatened, so she attacked it like an angry terrier, flinging the casements wide to drive out the scent of aftershave and the feel of him and being satisfied only when she had changed the bed-linen and the room smelled innocuously of fresh air and Vanno's lavender bags.

Afterwards, she returned to the kitchen, seated herself at the table and started on a letter to Martin, which she gave up after the fourth attempt. He had been a good friend to her and he was entitled to something better than a blunt 'I'm getting married shortly', which was all she could think of saying at the present. Maybe, when she had sorted out the right words, got them straight in her mind, she would phone him.

She looked at the telephone moodily and then ignored it, to leave the table and sit in Vanno's rocker and close her eyes, feeling tense and with only the steady ticking of the kitchen clock to break the silence around her. It was almost a relief when she heard a car draw up outside and the back door being flung open. Footsteps came along the hallway; light, swift footsteps which didn't hesitate. Ellis knew them instantly, she raised her head and lifted an eyebrow as the kitchen door was pushed open.

'Hello, Ellis.' Her foster-sister paused on the threshold, striking a top-model pose of languid elegance. 'You haven't changed a bit. How long has it been, four years?'

'Slightly longer.' Ellis corrected her gently but firmly; she wasn't exactly unforgiving, but Gwenny's two-year silence was a bit much to overlook, and besides, her foster-sister had the best of reasons for knowing exactly how long it was since they had last met; so why pretend? 'Davey was five last February,' she pointed out gravely.

'Don't remind me!' Gwenny gave a small but dramatic shudder and touched at the subject delicately, as if it might bite back at her. 'It was all so long ago, and sometimes I almost think I dreamed it all. Aren't you going to say you're glad to see me?'

'Of course I'm glad to see you, Gwenny.' Ellis was still slightly reproving, she felt she had justification, but then maybe so did Gwenny, who had been working for a living while she herself had been leading a comparatively idle life. One had to be fair. 'We've been expecting you ever since *Taid* died, and there's so much to tell you.'

'Don't tell me, let me guess.' Gwenny's smile was small and very controlled, barely concealing boredom. 'Dyffryn's become a sink of iniquity, the Chapel sale of work turned into an orgy and the schoolmaster's run off with a stripper. That should liven things up!'

'Nothing so exciting.' Ellis shook her head reprovingly. 'You've seen the schoolmaster's wife; the poor man wouldn't stand a chance. But Vanno had an accident and she's been in hospital for a week for tests and bed-rest. There's nothing for you to worry about, though, the doctor says her condition's not so serious that it can't be controlled; she just has to take life a little more slowly. Gideon wrote to you about it; he didn't want to frighten you with a cable. Haven't you had his letter?'

Absurdly, warning bells were ringing in her mind, making her feel nervous without any real reason. Gwenny was here and she, Ellis, should be glad, but a shiver of apprehension was making the hair on the back of her neck prickle so that her words came out huskily and she swallowed nervously while she took note of the changes in her foster-sister.

Gwenny had always been beautiful, but in the old days it had been a fierce, untamed beauty. Now it had been polished into utter perfection, with the fire of her hair tamed to a gleaming chestnut and with only the minimum of make-up to enhance the perfection of her features. Eyebrows and eyelashes had been tinted a bronzy colour, the faintest touch of green eyeshadow made the emerald of her almond-shaped eyes glow mysteriously, and her mouth was a pouting curve.

'I've been out of New York for a while, so I haven't had any letters for several weeks.' Gwenny shrugged elegantly. 'I suppose it'll be waiting for me when I get back.'

'Why didn't you let us know you were coming?

When did you arrive?' Ellis, wondering why she wasn't surprised when she should have been, made a move towards the cooker. 'Which will you have, tea or coffee?'

'Taking your questions one at a time,' Gwenny sauntered across to the table to toss her bag and gloves down on the breakfast cloth, 'first, my visit's a spur-of-the-moment thing. An offer out of the blue to do some modelling for a fashion house in London, expenses paid, including my air fare, so I thought I'd fly over a few days early and combine business with pleasure. Secondly, I flew into Manchester last night, hired a car at the airport this morning and drove straight here. Thirdly, I think I would be safer with tea. My experience at breakfast with hotel coffee was very off-putting, I thought they were trying to poison me. How do I look?'

She paused again before disposing herself on the settle, giving Ellis another chance to admire the picture she made. Tall, like all the Gruffydds; slender as a birch tree and with the same grace; Ellis felt reality slipping away from her. This was a new Gwenny, elegant, confident, sophisticated and with her beauty and impeccable grooming preserved beneath a rock-hard, transparent shell. She looked glossy, determined and vaguely discontented, like the pictures of her in the magazines. This was not the girl she had grown up with. In the place of that rumbustious teenager was a svelte, assured woman of the world.

'You look marvellous, but you always did.' Ellis paused with the teapot in her hand, pulled herself together and let her eyes range over an immaculate silk suit of the palest green, together with high-heeled shoes and accessories which either matched or contrasted exactly as they should, and at the huge emerald ring which drew attention to Gwenny's perfectly shaped hands.

'Looks aren't everything.' Gwenny's shrug was faintly discontented. 'But I have to keep up appearances. Only the very rich—like you—can afford to slop around eternally in off-the-peg blouses and skirts. I bet you even wear cotton underwear. I mean, can you honestly see me in anything so drab, even for travelling?'

'Not really.' Ellis was honest. 'You're well past that stage.'

'I was never *at* that stage, thank God!' Her foster-sister snapped it out and Ellis recalled the fights there used to be between Vanno and her daughter about what was and what was not suitable clothing for a teenager. Gwenny had always won those fights.

'I'll make the tea.' Ellis went about the little chore and spoke over her shoulder. 'Why didn't you phone or write? Vanno was very disappointed when you didn't, and now here's another disappointment for her. You've arrived and she and Davey have gone to Porthmadog with Gideon. I don't expect them back before teatime.'

'Davey! You've brought him here?' Gwenny's perfectly shaped mouth tightened with displeasure. 'Was that wise of you, Ellis?'

'Why not?' Ellis straightened her back and tilted her chin. 'I could hardly have come here without him, but you've no need to worry. I'm not a fool, and if I'd thought there was any possibility of somebody spotting a family resemblance, we wouldn't have come at all. He's just an ordinary little boy,' she continued quietly, 'who doesn't look like anybody but himself. You must have seen that already, I've sent you enough photographs.'

Gwenny wasn't mollified. 'I can't think why you came at all,' she grumbled, and Ellis's silver eyes sparkled with a fighting gleam.

'It was in the balance until Gideon came to London specially to tell me I wasn't welcome.' She made it sound humorous. 'A red rag to a bull,' she mused reflectively. 'You know how we always rubbed each other up the wrong way.'

'You haven't told anybody?' Gwenny let the question hang and Ellis was indignant.

'When did I ever break a promise to you?'

'Never that I can remember, but there's always a first time.' Gwenny was grudging for an instant before she became winning. 'Good little Ellis, I knew I could depend on you, but all the same I wish you hadn't left London. I was quite looking forward to parking myself on you and flaunting your prestigious address during the interview a weekly magazine has lined up for me.' She paused a moment before continuing blandly.

'You wouldn't object to a photographer taking a few pics of me inside the house, would you? One in the dining-room, for instance, with the table laid up for an intimate little party? So much more atmosphere than a studio set.' Gwenny went on blithely. 'It wouldn't be any bother to you,' she urged as Ellis registered a visible distaste, 'you needn't even come back with me if you don't want to. Just give me a key and I'll see that everything is tidied away and the house is safely locked up when we've finished.'

'I wouldn't give you the key to a dog kennel.' Ellis made a joke of it but the prickle of nervous tension in the back of her neck had increased so much she wanted to scratch it. 'I know how easily you lose things but,' she continued helpfully—because she had always helped Gwenny, 'I'll give you Martin's address. He has a complete set and he knows how to turn off and reset the burglar alarm, so he'll probably want to come with you.'

'Why?' Gwenny raised a haughty eyebrow. 'It's your house, isn't it? What has it to do with this Martin, whoever he is?'

'You've met him, I believe,' Ellis soothed. 'He came with Robert when you signed the adoption papers. He's our accountant, one of Davey's trustees and he's also my very good friend.'

'So that's the way the wind blows.' Gwenny's smile was still small but very understanding, almost a knowing leer. 'You must tell me all about him. Hurry up with that tea, Ellis. I'm dying of thirst.'

CHAPTER EIGHT

GWENNY was garrulous over unsugared, milkless tea and an unbuttered cracker, but like a barometer she went up and down with every change in the atmosphere.

'Success, Ellis; yes.' She grimaced slightly. 'I've been successful but it's like a desert mirage. You see it in the distance, you work your guts out to get to it but all you end up with is a handful of dollars which trickle away through your fingers.'

'You mean it's been a disappointment, not what you expected?' Ellis reached out a sympathetic hand but Gwenny ignored it to go on speaking, and Ellis heard her out in silence.

'Photographic models, the more famous ones, have a very short life.' Gwenny paused briefly, choosing her words with care. 'Close-up stills have a way of picking up the first signs of ageing: the little lines around the eyes, the slightest sag in the jawline; and the competition's fierce when you get to the top.' There was another pause and her green eyes became hard.

'One thing I've learned,' she continued flatly, 'it's a lousy way to earn a living. You have to look after your own interests, nobody does it for you. They build you up and suddenly, when you think you've got it made, they say your face is too familiar, that the public wants something new; somebody all fresh and dewy. And there she is, right behind you with all the arrogance of her seventeen or eighteen years; just waiting to push you off the top rung of the ladder it's taken you so long to climb. That's the time you go back to your apartment and take a good look at yourself and realise you're not young any longer.'

'But you're still beautiful,' Ellis protested.

'But I'm not *young*!' Gwenny was wry. 'And youth's what counts nowadays in the modelling racket. I'm a couple of years older than you, Ellis, nearly thirty, and the writing's on the wall, but,' Gwenny stopped glooming to become almost triumphant and a small smile of victory curved her lips, 'I've had another kind of offer and I'm off to LA in a month's time. It's only a small part in a TV soap, but it can lead to bigger things if I go about it in the right way.'

Her eyes had taken on a hard, ruthless gleam, and the set of her chin as she went on talking showed she was determined on that 'right way'. And when Gwenny was determined . . .

'Instant impact's the thing, Ellis, and if I don't manage that, I'll start small and stay small,' she continued hardily. 'At present, the plans are just for a few episodes until they write me out of the series, but I believe I'm worth more than that.'

'Of course you are.' Ellis was supportive. 'You're lovely to look at and you always were good at acting! Once you get your foot in the door . . .'

'I think so too.' Gwenny nodded complacently, 'so I *have* to make that impact, cause waves large enough to wash me right into the big time. I need to start off right: a luxury apartment, or better still my own house; a whole new wardrobe, a car, a maid, and, most important, the right kind of advance publicity; I have to be seen at the right places with the right people! All of which costs money, lots of it, so I thought of you. It's nice to have a rich relation, and since you owe everything you have to me, I've come to collect. I hope you've got your cheque-book handy!'

Ellis swallowed nervously. Was this what her doom-laden presentiment was all about? That deep down, Gwenny didn't care for anything or anybody but herself? With a sick feeling in her stomach—she had never been a match for her foster-sister, she never had been able to see only one side of a problem—she shook her head.

'If anybody owes, you do, Gwenny.' But she could hear her own voice and it didn't have the right crispness or decision. 'Robert gave you everything you asked for and he took your child, gave him a name and a secure future.'

'But he gave you so much more.' Gwenny said it sweetly but her eyes were hard with purpose. 'You don't understand, Ellis. That's your blind spot, your inability to see another person's point of view. Before Davey was born, your Robert told me he was thinking of marriage and that he was willing to adopt my child. So naturally, I thought he meant marriage to me, and why shouldn't I? All that talk about how much better it would be if the baby had a settled home with a father and mother. And he was so very generous, a trust fund for the baby, and I could have anything I wanted, but when it came to the crunch, it was you who walked off with the jackpot!'

'I'm sure Robert never misled you.' Ellis defended

her late husband stoutly. 'He would have laid it all on the line.'

'Maybe.' Gwenny shrugged defiantly and Ellis remembered that her foster-sister could never bear being put in the wrong. 'But one always hopes,' she continued hardily. 'Married to your Robert, I could have had the good life, moved in the top circles with not a care in the world, and I wouldn't have had to work for it! I'd have made something of being Robert's wife, whereas you . . .' She sniffed elegantly. 'You're wasted in the part. If he'd married any another woman, I wouldn't have minded so much, but to marry *you*! I'd never have signed those adoption papers if I'd known what he really intended. Your Robert tricked me, Ellis.'

'You should have married Gideon when he asked you.' Ellis said it wearily as she had said it so often in the weeks before Davey was born. 'You should have told him about the baby. Davey's his child and he wouldn't have let you down. He'd have put everything right and Vanno need never have known.'

'Marry a man who'd keep me here, in this dead-and-alive hole to vegetate?' Gwenny answered as she had always answered before, even when she was exhausted by Davey's birth and Ellis had pleaded again with her to tell Gideon. But no, Gwenny had been adamant, she would see it through on her own. But she hadn't!

'I wanted more out of life than that!' Gwenny was incisive, with a shrug which said burdens weren't for her. 'But that's all in the past,' she continued lightly. 'A bad dream and better forgotten. Most of the time, I can hardly believe it ever happened, so now let's get down to the nitty-gritty while we have the opportunity. It's so much easier to talk business wihout Mam breathing down my neck. She'd have killed the fatted calf, made a great fuss of me, and I wouldn't have been given the chance to talk to you as I'm doing now. You'll give me what I ask for, won't you? You could look on it as an investment.'

'I can't.' Ellis poured herself another cup of tea, it was stone cold and she didn't even notice. She was being made to feel again as she had felt when she was a child: unsure of herself, unsure of everything and overwhelmed by Gwenny's forceful personality.

'Of course there will be some money, if you really need it,' she continued, 'but not a lot, nowhere near what you seem to be asking for. To do what you plan would cost a fortune.'

'But that's just what you have, Ellis, isn't it? Something like a million? A fortune in anybody's language and,' her foster-sister's green eyes glittered like emerald chips, 'but for me, you wouldn't have had it. But for me, you'd still be a hard-working little secretary; slaving away from nine to five, shopping for bargain clothes in the sales during your lunch-hour and rushing home to your tatty little flat with a packet of fish and chips for your supper. *You* didn't have the baby, *you* didn't sweat with fear and pain, thinking every moment you were going to die. I tell you, I *earned* everything Robert gave me and a lot more besides!'

Ellis crowded down her misery. In a way, Gwenny was justified, Davey was *her* son but she still hadn't shown the least bit of interest in him, she hadn't even asked how he was, and that hurt. But at the same time, it stiffened Ellis's wilting backbone so that she could be firm. 'I couldn't give you more than five thousand, even if I wanted to.'

Gwenny raised an incredulous eyebrow. 'Don't be stupid! You're loaded, Ellis, and it's your money, isn't it?' Her mocking laughter rang in Ellis's ears like a peal of bells and the deriding quality of it seemed particularly inappropriate, so that Ellis's voice sharpened into nervous aggression.

'I've never looked on it as *my* money,' she scolded. 'Robert worked hard for it and he left very definite instructions with me about how he wanted it to be used. Besides, if I asked Martin to get me a really large amount, he'd asked why I wanted it, and I could hardly say I needed it because he knows I don't.'

'You may not need it, but I do.' Gwenny was completely relaxed but Ellis could sense the ferocious determination behind that relaxation. 'Tell Martin the truth, that it's for me, Davey's real mother. After all, he's only a hired hand, paid to do what you tell him. I'll give you a couple of days to think about it, but I'm sure you'll see it my way.'

'It wouldn't be what Robert wanted.' Ellis had no time to say more. Gwenny broke in furiously.

'To hell with what Robert wanted. He's dead and the money's yours now.' Abruptly, her temper died, but Gwenny had always been like that; mad as hell one minute and laughing the next. It was part and parcel of her magic. She was laughing now, a soft, throaty sound, and her green eyes glowed.

'Not that I wasn't grateful to him at the time,' she admitted. 'A mink coat; cases full of lovely, expensive clothes; a first-class flight to New York and enough cash to pay for a room at a classy hotel until I could afford a place of my own. I felt I could conquer the world . . . and I did! Now, is there anything to eat in this house?' She rose in one sinuous movement to go out into the scullery where the Calor-gas fridge was humming its head off.

'Oh, God!' Her voice came muffled, she evidently had her head in the fridge. 'Cold beef and potato salad, the calories will put pounds on me. Set the table, Ellis while I bring in the food. We'll have a nice gossip over lunch, just like the old days. Have you any news for me?'

And still not one word, not one little enquiry about Davey or Vanno. Ellis saw red and fumbled with a fresh tablecloth and the cutlery until the mist in front of her eyes cleared and she was able to think straight. Squabbling would get her nowhere, Gwenny was as impermeable as a fisherman's oilskins. No matter how hard you rained on her, she never got wet. She was, she always had been completely self-centred, but, in an odd way lovable with it.

The news that Gideon was considering giving away the Plas, and to whom, set her foster-sister's storm-signals flying again.

'He can't *do* that!' Gwenny squealed wrathfully. 'It's our family home, has been for generations.' She took a deep breath which thinned her aristocratically built nostrils. 'Now you tell me there could be a horde of scruffy little brats running all over it and doing untold damage. It doesn't bear thinking of.'

'It's either that or pull it down. Rates, repairs and running-costs, you know. Even if it's left empty, it has to be heated or it will just moulder away. It eats money.' Ellis maintained a cool front while a little question built up in her mind. Gideon's sum didn't add up. He'd said pull the place down or give it away or marry a rich wife, yet although he was marrying a rich wife, he was still considering giving the Plas away. It didn't make sense, not to her, but she supposed he had his reasons, and she didn't dare take time out to think about it now, not with Gwenny rattling on.

'He couldn't have pulled it all down, the *"hen"* is a listed building. We've our Nest to thank for that!' Gwenny had forgotten about being angry, she had relaxed, and Ellis fervently hoped she would stay that way.

'Your Nest and one of her more dubious offspring,' Ellis reminded her. 'You were always on about her when you were a kid.' She wrinkled her nose, remembering Gwenny's preoccupation with the old Wesh tale, part fact, part legend. 'I always thought it was mostly fiction.'

Gwenny waved aside fruit juice to drink water with the lean beef she was eating; she had also dismissed the potato salad as too fattening, especially now, when she couldn't afford to gain a single ounce. 'It's a true story,' she insisted obstinately. 'Just imagine, Ellis: a fifteenth-century woman who had the guts to leave her wealthy and noble husband because she'd fallen in love with another man. She gave up everything to run off with him and come and live here, in this God-forsaken hole.'

'You obviously haven't inherited her temperament.' Ellis was dry. 'But surely, it's not certain that she came here! Nearly every remote house in Wales, provided that it's old enough, lays claim to your Nest. There's a place outside Llangollen called

World's End, it's claimed she went there. And even if it *was* here, she didn't stay long; Pembroke and the fleshpots called.'

'Long enough to have a couple of kids,' and having made her point, Gwenny allowed herself another very small smile; wide smiles, even laughter encouraged wrinkles. 'But I've often wondered what tale she told her husband when he asked her where she'd been and what took her so long.'

'She went to visit her Mam and was caught up in the rush-hour traffic?' Ellis's dryness increased.

'You say the funniest things, Ellis,' Gwenny approved. 'You're quite wasted here. Tell you what, don't give me any money yet, just transfer a large chunk of it to a bank in the States and come back with me. You can be my secretary. I expect I shall need one to handle my appointments and there'll be a maid to look after my clothes. I might even run to a housekeeper if I can afford a house.'

'And Davey?' Ellis raised an eyebrow.

'Oh no!' Gwenny was definite. 'No kids, they spoil everything! We'll leave him here with Mam, you say she's fond of him and he'll be quite happy.' Thus Gwenny disposed of her son and Ellis knew a moment of blinding anger and had to clench her teeth to stop it pouring out in a vitriolic stream.

'No, I wouldn't go to America without Davey.' She was curt. 'Vanno's not well enough nowadays to cope with a child on her own, and besides, I have other plans. Gideon and I . . .'

'You and Gideon!' At the risk of a wrinkle in the smoothness of her forehead, Gwenny raised an eyebrow. 'You *do* surprise me, although I suppose he's only after the money. He always was a tight-fisted bastard. I used to have to steal from his cashbox if I wanted a magazine or a new pair of tights.' Her mouth curved into a droll moue. 'He kept it in one of the drawers of the desk in the office and he caught me red-handed the first time I did it.'

'What happened?'

'Nothing, of course.' Gwenny's eyes registered triumph. 'I said the first thing that came into my head. I told him you'd taken it to give to me and I was putting it back before it was missed. I cried a bit and said Mam must never know because she'd send you straight back to the orphanage. That was quite a good move, don't you think? Of course, being the first time, I didn't use my head.' Gwenny smiled craftily. 'I'd picked out all the notes and I must have had about a hundred pounds in my hand. But after that, I was wiser. I made sure nobody saw me and I only took small change. I didn't think he'd miss that.'

Ellis stared blankly ahead. Could this have been what had made Gideon distrust her? But Gwenny must be a fool if she thought he hadn't noticed her little thefts; his mind was like an adding-machine and he had a memory like an elephant. Then, she reminded herself that Gideon wouldn't have thought of them as Gwenny's thefts but as hers! No wonder he had despised her, he had thought she was a thief! Something inside her rebelled violently but common sense told her it was too late to do anything about it. Abruptly, she came back to the present, she had missed half of what Gwenny had been saying and had to make what sense she could of the remainder.

'I could put a stop to your romance, little foster-sister, any time I wish. Give me half an hour alone with Gideon and I guarantee he wouldn't even see you if he fell over you, so if it's Gideon you want, let's not waste any more time. Write me a cheque or pick up the phone and get on to whoever it is you need to get me some money. I have to have it and you can well afford . . .'

'*No!*' Ellis shocked herself with the violence of the word. For more years than she cared to remember she had made excuses for Gwenny, whom she had loved and admired since they had been children together, but now, that love and admiration had taken the most severe knock of all, and somewhere inside, Ellis was weeping a pool of disillusion. Gwenny's life was Gwenny, it was the way she was built! She was incapable of considering anybody else, not even Davey!

The atmosphere in the usually pleasant kitchen degenerated to the point where Ellis shivered and became wary, half wishing she had been less definite. It had never been any good trying to reason with her foster-sister, Gwenny had never been able to see any point of view but her own. And she had changed, become so much harder, more determined, and she wasn't asking, she was demanding. But when had she ever been able to deny Gwenny? Even now, she couldn't do that. She concealed her nervousness and made her voice firm.

'You're talking about a very large sum, tens of thousands of pounds. I can't just give you an amount like that, not without a lot of hassle.'

'You mean that, Ellis?' Gwenny slid sinuously to her feet and stood, tall, slender and elegant but without an atom of expression on her lovely face. It had gone back to being the model's icy mask, but her eyes were glittering with angry disappointment.

'Let me remind you of a few things,' she snapped. 'Mam brought you here when you were seven or eight; a workhouse brat, a charity child with nothing but the clothes you stood up in, not even a change of underwear or a spare pair of shoes. She housed, fed and clothed you for years, treated you as one of the family and made me share everything with you, even my bedroom.'

'As you said, an act of charity for which I was very grateful. I didn't realise you felt so resentful about it.' Ellis tried to remain cool, pretending to be unaffected, but it was difficult. Inside, she wept for a dream she had held on to for so long but which now seemed more like a nightmare. Gwenny had never loved her, only used her. 'Vanno was only being kind,' she added. 'She didn't love you any the less.'

'Oh, I know that.' Her foster-sister tossed her head and her green eyes glowed like a cat's. 'But it was you, Ellis! You were always so bloody prissy! "Ellis doesn't speak to me like that".' Gwenny's mimicry of her mother's voice was perfect, it could have been Vanno herself speaking. 'I hated your guts most of the time!'

'Sorry.' Ellis shook her head. The shock had numbed her, nothing Gwenny said now could hurt her more than she had been hurt already. She could even listen to the remainder of Gwenny's little tirade.

'Mam said you'd be good for me, make me learn to share.' Gwenny was letting everything spill out. 'She used to lecture me on Christian charity. Later, I realised she was right. You were so grateful, and when I was in real trouble with Davey, there you were running to help.'

'*You* ran to *me*,' Ellis reminded her. 'And it was the least I could do. I owed Vanno so much.'

'Then, "the least you can do" is repay the debt now,' Gwenny snorted in angry derision. 'You never did anything for my sake, did you? It was all for Mam. So she wouldn't be disappointed in me.' Abruptly her angry expression vanished to be replaced by a strange fierceness. 'But you've a proper sense of obligation, even if you *are* tight-fisted about the cash. Remember what I said: if it hadn't been for me . . .'

'You've made your point.' Ellis hung on grimly to her cool. Gwenny had always been like this, hurtful when she was angry or disappointed, but the mood never lasted long. 'I can give you a cheque right away but . . .'

'But it won't be a big one? Never mind, I'll look on it as a down-payment.' Her foster-sister raised a mocking eyebrow before all trace of her anger vanished to be replaced with a volatile, almost childish eagerness. 'How big?' she enquired greedily. 'Or should I ask how small? No, don't answer that; surprise me! Where do you keep your cheque-book?'

'In my bag.' Ellis nodded towards where it was hanging by its strap from the back of the settle. 'I'll just . . .'

'No.' Gwenny was already on her way, her high heels clicking on the quarry tiles like miniature explosions. 'I'll get it. Don't you dare move, Ellis;

you might change your mind.'

Ellis opened the bag which Gwenny slapped down on the table in front of her and riffled through the stubs in her cheque-book. 'If you need money straight away, I can't sign a cheque for more than five thou.'

'Six?' Gwenny bargained hopefully, but at the rueful shake of Ellis's head, she shrugged. 'Never mind, five will have to do for the present. Not enough for luxury,' she grumbled, 'but it'll part-pay for some publicity until you get me the second instalment, which shouldn't take long, I hope. What are you waiting for, hurry up and write it, Ellis, before you have second thoughts. I won't be really happy until you've signed it and I have it in my hand. Then, when I come tomorrow, all the preliminary business will be over and it'll be just a family visit. This,' she tossed a pasteboard slip on to the table, 'is the hotel where I'll be staying. I booked in by phone this morning and heaven knows what it'll be like; the pits, I suppose, but it's only for a couple of nights.'

'You're not staying here?' Ellis scribbled the cheque and handed it over, her worried eyes rounded with surprise so that she looked like a battered kitten; the blows were falling so thick and fast, she also felt like one. 'Oh, Gwenny; you can't do that, not to your own mother! She's been living for this moment. What on earth am I going to tell her when she gets home?'

Gwenny's green eyes widened into a look of innocence and she shook her head. 'Tut, tut, Ellis,' she drawled, 'what's happened to your brain, all turned to mush? You don't tell her about today, it never happened! When I come tomorrow, you'll both fall on my neck and weep tears of joy at seeing your beloved Gwenny for the first time in five years. You can leave the rest to me.'

'I couldn't do that!' Ellis was indignant.

'Why not?' Gwenny drawled it but her eyes sparked with amusement. 'I think it's by far the most sensible way. What Mam doesn't know won't hurt her.'

Ellis lifted her head and looked her foster-sister in the eyes steadily. 'What will you do if I can't get you any more money?' she enquired quietly and Gwenny shrugged.

'Steal Davey away from you, of course. Knowing you, you'll pay anything I ask to get him back!' And on a cloud of perfume, she wafted herself out of the kitchen and out of the house.

Ellis heard the slam of a car door and the roar of an engine which diminished into the distance. When the noise had at last died away, she sat brooding, looking at the table and the dirty dishes which covered it without really seeing anything, just letting the collywobbles in her stomach settle down before she even tried to work out the consequences.

A glance at her watch told her that only a little over two hours had passed since Gwenny's arrival but she checked again with the kitchen clock to make sure. So short a time and all her childhood memories and dreams had been shattered into little painful bits. Robert had always said that old dreams died hardest and today had proved him right. She had loved Gwenny, but all her foster-sister had ever felt was resentment.

But that was sheer exaggeration tinged with a hefty dollop of self-pity, she scolded herself. Today, Gwenny had been in a temper brought on by being thwarted. It had happened before, Gwenny had always gone from one extreme to another. When she cooled down it could be a very different story. But Ellis didn't dare take a chance on that, not when Davey's welfare and happiness were at stake. But that also was nonsense. Gwenny was Davey's mother, she *must* feel some love for him; mothers didn't hurt their children.

Only, Gwenny didn't want Davey, she had shown no interest in him, only in the money, so perhaps it would be wiser, safer if she, Ellis, took a longer view. He was only five, too young to be asked what he wanted now, but he would be given the chance later, so, until he was older, she, Ellis, would go on taking care of him.

Meanwhile—she could hardly believe so much had happened in so short a time, could she have imagined it all?—the sight of the table got through to her. The tea things, the two place-settings, the dirty dishes and glasses, Gwenny's crumpled napkin with a slight smear of lipstick to mar the snowy whiteness of the linen; it was all there.

It was useless to pretend nothing had happened, that she had dozed off and had a nightmare. It was all true, the demands, the threat, but just at present all she wanted to do was clear away all traces of it. Pulling herself to her feet and feeling unutterably weary, she loaded the dirty crockery and cutlery on to a tray, added the glasses and carried them into the scullery where she put them in the sink and turned on the tap.

Going to and fro, she washed up, restored order to the kitchen and scullery and finally bundled up the tablecloth to shake the crumbs out for the birds. It was all done automatically and she didn't even notice the small piece of white pasteboard which fluttered away in the freshening breeze.

Folding the cloth, she came back into the house and sat down while she considered what to do. Tell Vanno? Tell Gideon? And the answer to both was *no*! Maybe later, if everything else failed, she would tell Gideon. As the boy's father—even if he was unaware of it—he had a right to know; but Vanno, never! That had been her promise to both Gwenny and herself and she would keep it. So she had better do what she could to make everything safe and do it quickly.

Her hand was quite steady when she picked up the phone and dialled Martin's office and there wasn't even a tremble in her voice as she gave her name and asked the girl on the switchboard to connect her.

Martin came on the line and Ellis could almost see his blunt features set in his usual expression of good humour. It was a pity she had to wash that from his face but it couldn't be helped.

'Martin,' she began bluntly and continued in a matter-of-fact voice. 'Gwenny's been here today. She's over on a visit from the States and she wants money, rather a lot of it. I've given her a cheque for five thousand but she needs much more than that.'

'Then you're a bigger fool than I thought,' Martin interrupted, and she interrupted back, wishing she didn't have to hold this conversation over a telephone. It would have been much better face to face.

'I don't see how I could have avoided it.' Weary and worried, she became cross. 'Gwenny sounded quite determined, she said she'll take Davey if . . . She's returning to the States shortly, within the week, I think, so I've not very long to make the arrangements.'

'How much money?'

'Much, much more than I have in my private account. She wants to start over again in Los Angeles, make a big splash to impress the film world. She's had an offer, you see, and she needs so many things, clothes, a house, a car and especially a good publicity man. It'll cost the earth.' Ellis winced at the clatter as Martin dropped the phone. He must have picked it up at once because his voice came back to her, curt and final.

'No go! We'd need old Wimpole's agreement, which would slow things down, and in any case, I'd have to start selling out securities to get that sort of money in cash and this isn't the time to sell.'

'You might have to.' Ellis could feel herself going cold with an odd mixture of fright and determined. 'She's threatened to take Davey away from me and I can't let her do that. Yes, I know,' she cut in on Martin's splutter of disbelief, 'she doesn't really want him, it's maybe only a threat, but I don't like to take the chance.'

'She can't touch Davey,' Martin interrupted, but she cut in on his protest.

'That's what you think; I'm not so sure.' Ellis fought to steady her voice. 'Gwenny can be unpredictable, so please get that money. She's coming up to London in a couple of days, she's doing some modelling there and she wants to use the house. I've told her to come to you for the keys, and if you could give her the money at the same time.'

'Do what I can.' Martin was cynical. 'I'll also nail down the carpets and lock up the valuables. Meanwhile, I'll give you a bit of advice; don't let the boy out of your sight! Your foster-sister knows about his trust fund, Robert told her what he intended doing, and in my opinion, that's probably what she's after.' And she was nearly deafened as he dropped the phone back on the rest and left her staring at a piece of almost dead plastic which could only burr endlessly on an empty line.

CHAPTER NINE

FEELING older than Vanno, Ellis made herself a pot of tea, poured a cup and sat staring at it while it went cold, indulging herself in wishful thinking which didn't solve anything.

If only she had kept Davey with her today instead of sending him off with Vanno and Gideon. There was petrol in her car; she could have bundled him into it and driven off, left a note for Vanno and hidden herself and Davey away until the danger was over. Or, if only she'd been honest with Gideon in the first place; *made* him believe the truth about Davey, forced him to acknowledge the boy as his son! But she had been too worried about Vanno finding out, and there had been her promise to Gwenny . . .

Her mind ran on, mostly in ever-decreasing circles of regret, where the past and the present were inextricably mixed with a lot more 'if only's, until the low growl of the Land Rover brought her back to reality and she looked at her watch with disbelief. She even held it to her ear to make sure it hadn't gone mad. It was six o'clock already. A whole day gone with nothing to show for it, yet she felt as though she had done seven years' hard labour.

'No tea ready, Ellis?' Vanno reproved her as she took off her hat. 'We've had a lovely day; sunny and quite warm with not a drop of rain. What have you been doing?'

'Not much.' Ellis caught Davey up in a close embrace as he bounced around her with a mysterious parcel and Gideon, from the doorway, eyed her suspiciously.

' "Not much" doesn't seem to agree with you,' he gave his verdict. 'You look as though you've been buried and dug up again!' He was just as derogatory about her looks as Martin had been about her methods. There was no comfort in the whole world, nobody was being kind to her!

'I've a headache,' she grumbled, and realised it was true, only she had minimised it. She had the father and mother of a headache and she wished she were dead. Everything was falling apart and if anybody said one kind word to her, she'd howl! But she set Davey back on his feet and busied herself with laying the table in between listening to his attempts to tell her all he'd done.

'I paddled, Ellis. I took off my shoes and socks and paddled out in the sea for ever so far and the water was only up to my knees. And I had an ice-cream after my dinner and we went to a place with funny-looking houses and I brought you a present. Shall I open it for you? It's for flowers. I chose it and Aunty Vanno only helped a little bit.'

'Tea first,' she reminded him, 'and then I'll try to get the paper off without tearing it. It's such pretty paper.'

'Worried about the future, Ellis?' The meal was finished, Davey had been bathed and was in bed, Vanno was upstairs with him, telling him a bedtime story and Gideon seemed to have reverted to suspicion. He was looking at her pale face a little too closely with dark, keen eyes which saw far too much for her comfort.

'Me, worried?' She marched into the scullery with every appearance—she hoped—of a deliriously happy woman. 'What have I to worry about?' But when she reached the sink and turned on the taps, a sick feeling grew in her stomach and a little grimace of self-derision twisted her lips.

Why did things have to get so complicated? She only had to say a few words, but would he believe her? Or would he stop being half-way nice to her and revert to his old suspicious ways? With a trembling hand, she squirted washing-up liquid into the sink and watched as the water foamed. 'God says, take what you want—and pay for it!' and she wanted to marry Gideon, bear his children, live out the rest of her life with him; wanted it until the wanting was an ache that hurt unbearably. Would that be how she would have to pay: marry him and be suspected of anything and everything for the rest of her life?

She was no fool, she knew Gideon would be a good lover but she wanted more than that. She was greedy, she wanted all the trimmings. 'Get back to basics,' she told herself sternly. 'You're only doing this to get Davey his rights.' A bit more self-deception? Maybe she had started out that way but things had changed.

'I've been thinking about Vanno,' she digressed in a barely audible mutter, 'and I was talking to the builder recently about attaching a granny flat to the lodge.'

Gideon raised an eyebrow, 'Good thinking, but would Vanno . . .?'

'That's something I'll leave to you.' She was tart because it was either that or weep all over him. 'Your famous charm,' she added. 'Don't tell me you can't make it work on Vanno when everybody else falls down flat before it.'

'You don't,' he answered and, turning her head slightly, she caught a derisory glint in his eyes and a slight twist to his mouth which could have been self-mockery. 'What do I have to do,' he asked softly, 'to melt your hard heart?'

Make love to me, she wanted to shout. Trust me! Be kind and understanding. Put your arms round me and let me weep all over you. But she couldn't even say it, much less shout it. These last few days she had built a dream in which Gideon actually loved her. She *needed* that dream; at present, it was all that made the situation tolerable. So she kept her head down and scrubbed viciously at the forks until she felt the grasp of his fingers firm on her shoulder and she was turned to face him.

'Having second thoughts, *cariad*?'

'Second, third, fourth and fifth,' she gloomed, keeping her face averted, but it didn't work. He slipped his free hand under her chin to force her face gently round and upwards. Unbidden tears swam in her eyes so that his features were a blur. 'It's the decision-making and the waiting after the decision's been made.' She said it bitterly. 'I should have gone to bed with you when you asked me.'

'But I believe I'd have been disappointed if you'd agreed,' he said. 'It would have been too easy, not a bit like you. Although I'd have taken anything you offered,' he added honestly.

Ellis raised a tear-smudged face and gazed at him wonderingly with eyes dulled from silver to pewter-grey. 'You'd have been disappointed in *me!*' she sniffed. 'Aren't I the villainess of the piece; only out for what I can get or steal?'

'Are you?' The lift of his dark eyebrow set her heart hammering.

'What if I am?' she blustered.

'Somehow, you don't seem to fit the part nowadays. Perhaps we both needed time to re-evaluate each other.' He murmured it into her hair as he pulled her closer and his mouth hovered a bare inch above hers. But it only hovered, it didn't make contact, and she almost screamed with disappointment. 'You've had a lonely day, too much time to think. Go to bed and sleep, *cariad*; it'll all look different in the morning, and by the way, throw out that new perfume you've been experimenting with. It doesn't suit you.'

'Not my perfume, Gwenny's.' The chance had been there for her to say it but she couldn't bring herself to take it.

She slept badly. What time she wasn't awake, worrying—which seemed to be the greater part of the night—her fitful sleep was crowded with nightmarish dreams. In them, Davey was always receding from her, no matter how hard she ran to catch him, and Gwenny's mocking laughter rang so loudly in Ellis's mind that it woke her and she had to get out of bed and stumble to Davey's bedside to make sure he was still there.

There was another nightmare as well. In that one, she was sitting on a hillside under a lowering sky, with a suitcase full of money. Bundles and bundles of notes packed in tightly but as she opened the case to show Gwenny, the notes either blew away or rain came falling to turn them all into worthless pulp. Martin haunted her also with his brusque 'Don't let him out of your sight' and she could hear herself whimpering with fear because she couldn't run fast enough to catch up with an elusive Davey.

She was exhausted and covered with a cold dew of perspiration when morning finally dawned, and after a suitable delay, while she lay on her side, watching the small, sleeping hump in the other bed and trying to be reasonable, she made her way to the bathroom and peered owlishly in the mirror. There were dark circles under her eyes; she looked as though she had been awake for a week, and although she took a coolish bath plus a furious scrub with Vanno's long-handled bath-brush, it did absolutely nothing for her.

Hurriedly, she towelled herself dry, returned to the bedroom and dressed in another of the blouses and skirts which Gwenny despised so much. She wasn't fashionable, only neat, she gloomed as she brushed her silvery hair—perhaps it wasn't so much silver as white with worry—into its usual French pleat and skewered it safely with far more hairpins than usual. No wonder Gideon didn't love her, had only ever offered her a romp in bed to take his mind off his worry. In the dark, one woman was very much like another.

'You're going out of your tiny little mind,' she told her reflection forcefully, 'so pull yourself together,' but her reflection merely sneered back at her, hollow-eyed and putty-faced. A dab with a powder-puff wasn't going to be enough this morning, and she set to work with a tube of tinted foundation and a blusher.

When she had finished, she looked quite colourful and healthy, she even practised a small smile which didn't look too artificial. It boosted her sagging morale and the time she had taken over the task had nicely used up at least half an hour. She could hear Vanno and Gideon downstairs in the kitchen and the rattle of crockery, plus the aroma of frying bacon, and it was time to wake Davey.

'Whassa matter, Ellis?' he demanded as she practically hauled him out of bed and hustled him into the bathroom. 'Are we going somewhere speshul 'cos Idris is coming? But I want to see my dog first. I didn't see him yestiday.'

'No, we're not going anywhere special.' Ellis forced herself not to shout, or worse still, burst into tears. 'And when Idris comes, we'll both take you to see your dog, I promise.'

'But me and Idris . . .' Davey's lower lip became mutinous; he had been looking forward to an extended playtime with his puppy and if Ellis was there, she would probably hurry him away. Ellis took the hint.

'I want to see the pup as well.' She was reasonable, even encouraging. 'If he's going to live with us, he'd better get to know me so's he won't be lonely when you go to school. Now, I'll run your bath and you must wash yourself properly while I get your clean clothes.'

'I shall be washed away.' Davey chose this morning of all mornings to be obstreperous. 'Idris only has a bath every other day; he said too many baths was bad for me. Why do I have to . . .?'

'Because I say so,' Ellis tried not to sound cross as she tested the water, found it too hot and turned on the cold tap. 'And it's less messy,' she added. 'Remember your ears, don't slop water all over the floor,' she concluded, 'and keep the soap in the tray or it'll dissolve.' And she went back to the bedroom, trying to be oblivious to Davey's loud chant.

'Ellis is cross this morning.' He was shouting it at the top of his voice and squeezing his pastic boat so that it hooted and gurgled.

And he didn't stop there! In typically childish fashion, he objected to the clothes she brought him. 'Thass my Sunday shirt and trowsis and it's only Satiday,' he complained. 'Now, I can't play with my dog. You said I mustn't sit on the ground in my best trowsis . . .'

'Today you may,' Ellis was nearly in tears of frustration; her bad night had sapped her energy so that she threw caution to the winds. 'You've nearly grown out of them, so you can sit on the ground and play with your dog in your best trousers. You can let him make a mess of your best shirt, you can kick lumps out of your best shoes and get your best socks dirty as well. You can do anything you like as long as you hurry up. Auntie Vanno will have breakfast ready and we mustn't be late.'

'Why?'

'Because!' she answered him distractedly as she hauled him out of the bath and towelled him dry.

Usually so good, the devil was in him this morning and he fought her every inch of the way, but at last he was clothed and she menaced him with the hairbrush.

'I want short hair, like Idris. Cut it *now*. Ellis, so's I don't have curls and look like a girl.'

'I'll do better than that,' she promised wildly. 'Next week, I'll take you to the barber and tell him to turn you into a skinhead!' But when she at last convoyed Davey downstairs, disappointment dropped on her like a thick, stifling cloak; Vanno was alone in the kitchen, Gideon had gone. Which was a disappointment because, part-way down the stairs, she had half made up her mind to break her promise and tell him the truth about Davey.

Not in front of either Vanno or the boy, of course, but she could have found some excuse to get him on his own. Now, she would never know whether or not she would have had the courage. 'Fool,' she scolded herself, 'he wouldn't have believed you. What's your angle, trying to get in his good books? Fat chance you have of doing that,' and she swept the disappointment from her face to return Vanno's greeting and be over-cheerful as she looked round the kitchen.

'Where's our wandering boy this morning? Gone with his doggie to harry another flock of poor little sheep?'

'N-no.' Even Vanno seemed a bit put out. 'He went out to check the Land Rover, he had a bit of trouble with it yesterday. Then he came back to tell me he was off, and I'd been looking forward to a talk with you both this morning.'

'What about?' Ellis tried to look mystified. She wasn't very successful because Vanno snorted.

'You know very well what about,' she snapped crossly. 'I may be old but I'm not blind; well, not for long; or stupid!' Her eyes slid to where Davey had scrambled on to his chair and was waiting, spoon poised for somebody to fill his cereal bowl. 'But that's your own business,' she continued in a lower voice. 'Yours and Gideon's, although why you didn't tell him about Davey years ago, before the child was born, defeats me! He would have married you, I'd have seen to that! Wicked at times he can be, but he'd not knowingly allow his child to be fathered by another man. And if you didn't want to tell him, you could at least have told *me*!' she added in a frustrated mutter: 'Leaving me in the dark all these years . . .'

Ellis spilled cornflakes into Davey's bowl and added milk before she growled, 'Damn Gideon, Vanno. He'd no right . . .'

'Who has a better?' Her foster-mother's dark eyes sparkled with the unaccustomed brightness of unshed tears, although she continued in the same low voice, never letting it rise enough that Davey might hear and understand. 'And when I think of you turning to a stranger for help . . . I can understand you not telling Gideon, although I consider it wilful pride, but you could have told me! What had I ever done that you should be afraid of me?'

'I've never been afraid of you, Vanno.' Ellis looked wry. It seemed so odd, almost unjust to defend herself, not with lies but with the truth, she had invariably known when she was being lied to so perhaps it was better this way.

'You gave me everything,' she continued softly, 'I just didn't want to hurt you or *Taid*. Besides, what right had I to burden you with my troubles? You'd already done enough for me. And Robert wasn't a stranger,' she continued quietly. 'Not to me. I'd been working for him for more than a year so I knew the kind of man he was. I admired and respected him. He offered me marriage and a home, he said he would adopt Davey legally . . .'

'Silly girl.' Vanno patted away the moisture from her eyes with a corner of her morning apron. 'You could have kept Davey here just as well as in London, and if you didn't want to marry Gideon, at least the boy would have been with his own family. You wouldn't have been the first girl to get into that situation and you won't be the last, but Davey's Gideon's.' Vanno was obstinate. 'You should have told either him or me, not your employer.'

'You weren't there, and I wasn't sure if either of you would want to know.' Ellis—by this time thoroughly tired of half-truths—prayed she wouldn't run out of excuses.

'Of course I'd have wanted to know!' Vanno was indignant. 'How could you, Ellis; treat me as if I were a stranger?'

'I'm sorry,' and Ellis was, genuinely! 'Yes, of course I should have told you, but long ago I promised myself I'd never worry you, and you would have been worried, you *know* you would. I didn't exactly lie in my letters,' she added wryly. 'I just didn't tell you all the truth. I suppose I wanted you to think well of me.'

'Humph,' Vanno snorted down the slightly hooked but aristocratic nose she shared with all the other Gruffydds, both male and female. 'Truth will out,' she added sententiously before her face broke into a rather watery smile. 'I should have known as soon as I saw the boy, but then, I didn't think . . . Never mind, though, Gideon's straightened everything out and he tells me you're getting married. I'm not having any hole-in-the-corner business, mind you. You'll have a proper wedding.'

Ellis breathed a sigh of relief. No more questions she couldn't answer without lying her head off, and her thoughts slid to Gideon. He must have told quite a good story, all lies, but she could go along with it and still keep her promise to Gwenny; Vanno's health might not be good enough to take another, bigger shock. She looked at her foster-mother gravely, watched her as she bustled about; frying bacon, breaking eggs swiftly and competently and petting Davey when, his cereal eaten, he slid from his chair and went to stand beside Vanno and make sure that his bacon was crisp as he like it and that his poached egg wasn't runny.

Idris appeared at the back door, just in time for toast and marmalade, and Vanno spread the butter thickly before grimacing as she scraped a very little of the low-cholesterol spread on to her own portion of toast; hastily covering the stuff with far too much marmalade so that she wouldn't taste it. Idris, with a polite 'Good morning, Mem,' to Ellis and a '*Bore da*' and a delighted '*Diolch yn fawr*' to Vanno, obeyed her gesture to pull up a chair.

'Bring him a plate, Ellis,' Vanno ordered in the old, comfortable way. 'He'll have had his breakfast but I don't suppose a bit more will hurt him. He's a growing boy and he's already walked several miles, he'll be as empty as a drum. Better make some more toast, though, or we shan't have any for ourselves. And that reminds me: Gideon's taken your car, not the Land Rover; he said to tell you.'

'Amazing!' Ellis manufactured a bright smile. Another exit sealed against her but troubles didn't disappear if you ran away from them, they lurked on the edge of your mind and coloured everything dark. 'I bought that car specially so I'd have transport but it hasn't seemed to work that way. Gideon's a pest!' and she offered the last piece of toast to Idris as if everything were perfectly normal and she didn't want to get down on her hands and knees and bite the hearthrug to pieces. Maybe she wouldn't have run away, but she would have liked to have the chance!

Hastily, she mopped marmalade from Davey's hands with the wet dishcloth and scolded him gently because he had developed an overwhelming interest in Idris's boots, which looked as though they could yomp all the way to Plynlimmon and back. From the unusually covetous look in his eyes, he was going to ask if he might have boots just like that.

'Mam says for Davey to have dinner with us,' Idris's English was quaintly slurred with a lot of hissing about the 'says' and 'us'. 'We will take the pushchair, pleass. He iss too small to walk all the way and after dinner, I will take him for a walk and I will bring him back thiss afternoon.'

'See my dog first.' Davey had a one-track mind, but to him any change in routine was an adventure and Idris had evidently taken upon himself the role of watchdog over an ignorant 'Saessneg hogyn'.

'That will be nice for you, Davey.' Vanno bustled about to wrap a new loaf of bara brith in a spotless napkin—Davey had developed a liking for the well-buttered Welsh currant bread—and threw Ellis a heartening look.

'Go with them as far as the *"hen"*, Ellis, the walk'll do you good, and Davey will be quite safe with Idris. One of a big family, you know, and quite used to looking after the younger children, what time he isn't helping his father with the sheep. Come back here for your tea, Idris,' she added. 'The bara brith's for your Mam but I'll have hot scones ready for you and maybe some custard tarts.'

And Ellis couldn't say no, that she would wait for Gwenny, because she wasn't supposed to know Gwenny was coming. But this way would be safer, she would be obeying instructions. Martin's curt 'Don't let him out of your sight!'

'You'll be all right on your own?' She hesitated, 'You won't do anything mad like overwork or fall down the stairs again?'

'Of course not!' Vanno's smile lit her dark eyes to beauty. 'I shall make myself one more slice of toast and, if I feel reckless, I shall have real butter on it. After that, I've a few letters to write and some knitting to finish.' Her look of innocence was pathetic. 'Will you be cross if I do a bit of cooking?'

Davey insisted that his pup had grown. It came to meet him as Ellis pushed open the door of the *'hen'* and he scooped it up and held it jealously as if it might be ripped from his arms at any moment. He became quite deaf when Ellis, intent on sticking to him like glue, said they had a long way to walk, so she sat on a heap of straw behind a bulwark of bales of the stuff and yawned while she waited. Now that the sun was shining, and the '*hen*' was quite cosy and protected from the draught by the low wall of bales, she was almost warm. The bitch was nowhere to be seen, but one adventurous pup came to sprawl across her ankles and chew her shoelaces.

She closed her eyes and relaxed while she listened to Davey's excited chatter and Idris's slower speech. Just closing her eyes for a few moments wouldn't hurt, and they'd tell her when they were ready to leave.

Ellis woke from a happy dream, opened her eyes on unfamiliarity and took several moments to orientate herself. She was still in her nest of straw but now two pups were fighting over which could rip her shoelaces to pieces, but otherwise everything was quiet, too quiet. There was no sound of the boys but when she peeped over the bales, she could see, outlined in the open doorway, a tall, black silhouette. She blinked at it.

'Looking for something, Ellis?' Gideon questioned mockingly as he carefully closed the door and strode towards her; as though he liked to see her hot and bothered. She lifted her chin and hoped she didn't sound too concerned.

'Only Davey,' she paused, feigning unconcern. 'He's gone off with Idris, I suppose.' She shrugged and went on the attack. 'Thank you for taking my car just when I needed it. I don't know why I bothered to buy it, I might just as well have come by train!'

Gideon ignored the bit about the car; instead, he raised his eyebrows. 'And you were asleep when they went off?'

'Oh, go to hell!' Ellis wiped cold perspiration from her forehead. His abrupt change in manner confused her. Last night he had been so easy to get on with and now it was all changed, but two people could play that game. 'Where are they now?' she demanded and if there was the suspicion of a panic in her voice she tried to cover it with a belligerent snarl.

But Gideon caught the sound of it and the amused mockery returned to his voice. 'Not much of a caring parent, are you, Ellis? But then, I can hardly call you a parent at all, can I?'

'I beg your pardon?' Ellis managed an icy surface to her confusion and he gave her a hard look and an even harder laugh.

'Stop playing games, girl. Do you think I'm blind? From the first time I saw Davey, something about him intrigued me. I couldn't pin it down at first, it was so fleeting, but I saw it clearly at Ynyslas when he came charging at me, accusing me of hurting you. It's uncanny how the very young and very old can look so alike. He was a miniature of *Taid* in a temper!' He smiled down at her fiendishly while he demolished her last hope. 'No, we're not hurrying back! I told Vanno you were dragging your feet and that I'd have a word with you in private.' At last Ellis knew the full meaning of the phrase 'a pregnant pause'.

'We Gruffydds,' he continued blandly, 'used to be a big family. Now, we're reduced to just three: Vanno, Gwenny and myself, four if you count Davey. So if you—no relative at all—are Davey's mother, I'd have to be his father, wouldn't I? And we both know that's impossible!'

'Put that in writing, sign it and I'll get it framed to hang on the wall,' she answered angrily. 'I spent most of breakfast-time being forgiven, although you didn't escape entirely unscathed!'

That made him chuckle and he slid down on to the straw beside her, putting his arm about her shoulders. 'Vanno been getting at you? Poor Ellis,' he mourned. 'Do you still insist you're Davey's mother?'

'Not any longer—not to you!' Ellis tried to brazen it out. 'The fairies brought him. What else!'

Gideon shook his head at her helplessly. 'Why, just for once, won't you tell the truth? Try it, you'll find me very understanding. For instance,' he groped in a side pocket of his jacket and produced a piece of rather battered white pasteboard. 'Would you care to explain this?'

For a moment, Ellis stared blankly before her memory started to work overtime and she recalled Gwenny tossing down just such a card: 'This is where I'm staying.' She tried to remember what she had done with it but she couldn't even recall picking it up.

'Underneath the Land Rover.' Taking pity on her agonised expression, he answered the question she hadn't asked. 'I found it when I went out early to see what was wrong with the exhaust. This card is new, it couldn't have been on the yard long. You had a visitor!'

Ellis ground her teeth. Tripped up by such a little thing; how could she have been so *stupid*! She hunted around for an adequate explanation but her brain had turned to mush. 'Martin . . .' she quavered as a last resort.

'Not unless he wears a see-through nightie and that perfume I noticed last evening.' Gideon's voice quivered with amusement and it was as if all his body were shaking with laughter. ' ''See how she twists and turns",' he quoted, missing the bit about avoiding fate and continuing warningly, ' ''Step lightly, lady!'' '

'I don't know what you're talking about,' Ellis pretended, not very well, to innocence. 'If you'd just put it plainly, in words of one syllable,' but his reply was another snort of stifled laughter. Gideon laughing! At her! Ellis could hardly believe her ears, but that laughter emboldened her so that the cramps of fear in her stomach died away only to be resurrected by his next remark.

'You'll have to do better than that, *cariad*, I want the truth! That tale you told at breakfast yesterday—about having to wait for a telephone call—was as weak as water but I went along with it; I thought you needed time to yourself. But when I found that card this morning, it gave me ideas.'

'Nothing unusual in that,' she interrupted. 'You're always having ideas about me, usually foul ones.'

'Don't interrupt while I'm trying to explain,' he reprimanded her. 'You make me lose the thread but, to continue. I checked your petrol gauge to see if you'd used your car and you hadn't, so I reasoned that, if you hadn't been out, somebody must have called. And, driven by a dark suspicion that my wife-to-be was up to something behind my back, like running away . . .!'

'Pooh!' she broke in on him. 'Why should I do that? I'm no shrinking virgin, frightened out of my skin by old wives' tales of the dreadful things a man does to his bride on their wedding night.'

'Shut up!' His hand came across her mouth, effectively silencing her, and she wondered if she could get her jaws open wide enough to bite his fingers. Then she realised she was really enjoying this battle of wits, would be happy for it to go on for a long time, only there was danger in that.

'So I took your car,' Gideon continued softly, too softly, 'and I drove down to that hotel this morning and as proof, I've brought you another memento.'

Her mouth was freed as he reached into another pocket and his hand came out holding her cheque for five thousand pounds which he waved under her nose.

'I'll have to cure you of being secretive and far too liberal with money, even if it is your own,' Gideon mused aloud with a woeful shake of his head. 'Nowadays, I can afford a decent standard of living, even a few luxuries, but I draw the line at your subscribing to this particular charity! So, are you going to tell me the truth? I think it's time you did!'

CHAPTER TEN

'SO that's why you pinched my car this morning.' Ellis needed time to think. He had seen and talked to Gwenny but she wouldn't have parted either with information or that cheque easily, and Ellis wondered what methods Gideon had employed. Strong-arm tactics or seduction? The thought of either made her so jealous there was no room left for worry or nervousness.

'Interfering in my private affairs again!' She went on the attack. 'You're too nosey, Gideon. Poor darling!' She pretended a syrupy sympathy. 'Looking for my dark secrets and finding . . .' she paused provocatively '. . . only Gwenny!'

Gideon's hard look was almost a leer. 'But Gwenny spilled the beans, my little dear. But, as I suspected most of it already . . .'

'Well, she would, if you bullied her.' Ellis brazened it out and hoped for the best.

'It was noisy,' he admitted with a knowing grin. 'Raised voices, even hysteria; but I didn't bully her. I only slapped her bottom. I've a good mind to slap yours, Ellis! Playing God; deceiving Vanno, bringing her grandson here and passing him off as your own.'

So he knew some of it, but how much? Ellis tried to think of something intelligent to say. 'Vanno knows now that Davey's a Gruffydd so does it matter if she's got it wrong and thinks he's ours? If you

171

remember,' she added cattily, 'I didn't give her that impression, you did!'

'No, it isn't enough,' he interrupted. 'She has a right to know the truth, and I've an even better right! And there's something else,' he added threateningly. 'This cheque for five thousand pounds. Has Gwenny *sold* you the boy?'

'No,' Ellis sighed. The moment of truth at last and she still wasn't prepared for it. But not all the story, not yet! She would save the best bit, let him have it as a parting shot, with the accent on 'parting'. 'You won't like it,' she added warningly. She couldn't expect Gideon to be delighted, but at least he might revert to being half-way human.

'Let me be the judge of that!'

'On your head be it.' She shrugged while her mind skated round, condensing and cutting out anything even remotely unpleasant until the drab little tale was quite clear in her mind; clear, precise and innocuous. 'Gwenny came to me when she knew she was pregnant,' she began, and continued in a voice completely devoid of emotion. She was surprised at how short a time it took, and Gideon listened without interrupting. 'Satisfied?' she asked when she had finished.

'Not completely.' He was scowling now. 'Why go to you for help? Why didn't she just come home? What had you to offer her?'

'Anonymity.' Again Ellis shrugged. 'She didn't want to hurt Vanno and besides, here, everybody would have known. She was newsworthy even then and it could easily have got out, which might have damaged her career. Some firms are very choosy about the models used in their advertisements. But you can hide in London, if you want to. You live in a flat, keep to yourself and after a while, nobody even sees you. You could die and nobody would know until the rent was overdue,' she added disgustedly.

'But she told your husband?'

'No, she didn't!' Ellis said with a sweetly sour smile. 'I did! Only at the time, he was only my employer; the man who paid me to work for him and,' she caught the faint wrinkle of Gideon's nose, as though there were a bad smell under it, 'that's the truth. We had a simple business relationship, nothing else. Believe me, all men aren't oversexed and not every girl is willing to leap into bed!'

'If your relationship was so businesslike, why tell him at all?'

'Grr!' Ellis showed her teeth. 'A matter of pounds and pence! I'd had to take time off quite often to be with Gwenny and Robert was threatening me with a doctor to cure my "sick headaches". He'd have soon found out there was nothing wrong with me, and I *needed* to keep that job.' She tilted her chin defiantly. 'Two can't live as cheaply as one, no matter what the book says.'

'And after the baby was born, your Robert adopted him and Gwenny went off to America. Where did she get the money for that; from your Robert?'

'No!' Ellis nearly strangled herself being emphatic as she remembered Gwenny's tale of a spending spree. 'With the adoption pending, his QC advised against that. But Robert helped in other ways. Gwenny'd told him how much she wanted to work in the States and he had friends everywhere. He could pull strings if he wished and I believe he fixed it so that she could work with a photographer he knew in New York. I think,' she added diplomatically, 'he did give her a bit of cash to pay for a place to stay until she could afford an apartment of her own.'

'And where did you come in on all these arrangements?' Gideon was probably checking to see whether her account and Gwenny's tallied.

'Nowhere!' She shrugged and bent the truth all the way as the old instinct to protect Gwenny surfaced. Even real sisters often fell out, said horrid things to each other, but it was never more than a storm in a teacup. 'Not until Robert and I were married, and that was the week after Gwenny left.'

'What a mess!' Gideon nostrils twitched fastidiously. 'Now tell me about this cheque.'

'Gwenny needs some extra money.' Again Ellis shrugged. 'She's branching out into films and she wants to make an impact. End of story.' But there was still the one salient point she had left out because, fortunately, Gideon hadn't asked that question yet. 'Any more questions?' She raised her chin defiantly. 'I'm quite willing to answer them, but please may we go and see Davey first? He can't be far away and afterwards, I'll talk my head off. I worry about him.' Ellis felt Gideon's arm tighten about her.

'Yet you let him go off alone.'

'I didn't let him go anywhere alone.' She was indignant. 'He's with Idris. We were all going down to Idris's Mam's, we only called here on the way, and I dozed off while they were playing with the pups.'

'Guilty conscience keeping you awake at night?'

'I do not have a guilty conscience,' she protested

vigorously. 'Let me go, you—you bully; I don't have to explain anything to you!' But she might as well have shouted at the stones in the walls to fall down, the arm about her didn't slacken by one iota.

'If he's with Idris, he'll be quite safe.' Gideon wasn't shouting as she had shouted. His voice was quiet but his mouth was set in an implacable line. 'We've still a few things to clear up.'

'But I must!' she interrupted violently, turning in his arm so that she had her back to him. She struggled against his grip and, when it didn't loosen, she elbowed him hard, in the stomach.

Gideon absorbed the blow with a stifled grunt but its effect was not what she expected. He was laughing as his hold slackened.

'Damn sharp little elbows you have, Ellis. They say it's the sign of a born scold.' She was at a disadvantage now because she could no longer see his face. She squirmed as she felt his hand invade her jacket and come to rest on her small breast. Through the thin material of her shirt she could feel him cupping it as though he were estimating the weight, and after that his fingers began a gentle massage which blew her mind.

'Don't do that!' she squalled angrily and straw crackled as she drummed her heels. 'I won't be fondled as if I were a tart!'

'It distracts you?'

'Yes, damn you. That's why you did it.' She gritted her teeth. 'I want to see Davey, *now*!' she added in a surly fashion.

'But I've still a few questions.' His breath tickled the back of her neck. 'He'll be quite safe with Idris.

Now that we've time to ourselves, you'd better tell me the rest of it. Who is his father? Gwenny must have told you.'

'Oh, she told me!' For this moment, Ellis had been waiting nearly three long years, ever since Robert had died. She had rehearsed it often enough to be word-perfect when the time came, but it was all going wrong. Gideon shouldn't have had to ask that question.

Somehow, there wasn't the right taste of triumph in her mouth and the words lacked conviction. She said them because they were what she had believed for so long.

'You are, Gideon.' She even heard the slightly questioning rise to her voice and tried again. 'You *are*! Gwenny told me.'

'You're sure of that?' He was very still and she hurried into her answer.

'Quite sure.' She felt oddly breathless. 'She told me so. You proposed and she refused, but she didn't know she was pregnant. It's why I brought Davey here,' she gabbled, keeping her eyes fixed on the old stone wall in front of her. She essayed a laugh which got stuck in her throat and emerged as a whimper of misery. 'Every boy needs a father-figure, and who better than his real father?'

'Sorry to contradict a lady.' He said it angrily to the back of her neck. 'But you've been misinformed! I've never proposed to Gwenny and I am *not* Davey's father!'

No reasons, no excuses; only a flat denial. Ellis shook her head, trying to get some order into her thoughts. 'Gwenny said you were,' she protested but even to her own ears, she sounded less than sure. 'Why should I believe you in preference to her?'

'No reason at all,' he said quietly into her ear and she shivered as his breath stirred the hairs on the back of her neck. 'But I hope you will,' he added gently. 'Had things been different, I might have been his father; the opportunity arose. I can only say that I am not.'

'You weren't lovers?' Ellis stared bleakly at the wall.

'I only said the opportunity arose.' Gideon's voice was curt and somehow as old as the stones she was staring at. 'I came down to London. We met, we went back to my hotel for dinner.' Ellis heard his almost sighing breath before he continued flatly, 'End of story!'

Ellis winced at the way he had said it! It had an unmistakable ring of truth, but she needed time to adjust to it.

'This morning,' Gideon sounded reluctant, 'when I asked Gwenny the same question, she refused to name the man but she did say that Davey's father was dead, killed in a car crash. For some reason, I assumed she meant your Robert. That was how he died, wasn't it? And from what you've said, he was suspiciously helpful to Gwenny.'

Such an easy way out, and for a second, she was tempted to take it. Robert wouldn't have minded, he would probably have applauded her ingenuity. 'Fiction's easy,' he had often said. 'You tailor it to fit the plot.' But this wasn't fiction.

'Then you assumed wrongly,' she said firmly. 'Robert had always wanted a child. If he'd been the father, he'd have made Gwenny marry him and she could have gone her own way afterwards at his expense. Only Davey would have mattered to him.' And she hoped that would be enough. She was determined not to explain about Robert's inadequacy; she owed him too much, respected him too much to do that.

'Then who . . .?' It had been enough but Gideon was worrying at it like a dog with a bone and Ellis felt her temper slipping.

'How should I know?' she snapped. 'I've never given it a thought since Gwenny told me it was you. She volunteered the information, and I saw no reason to doubt her. Besides, he looks a bit like you sometimes!'

'Stupid!' Gideon snorted. 'He looks like a Gruffydd and that's just what Gwenny is, despite her red hair and green eyes.'

'Then what's the hassle?' she asked. 'Oh, for heaven's sake! Davey's a nice little boy, we know his mother, what else matters?'

'But if not Robert then who?' Gideon wouldn't leave it alone, 'You must have some idea.'

'No, I haven't.' Ellis was almost weeping as with flailing arms she fought herself round to face him and beat at his chest with small, ineffectual fists. 'Gwenny told me one thing, now you tell me she tells you another. I'm at the stage where I don't know what or who to believe any longer, except that I know it wasn't Robert!'

'Your Robert must have been quite a man to have earned so much loyalty, Ellis.' The unshed tears were too thick in her eyes for her to be able to see his face properly but she could hear the wry note in his voice. 'A better man than I am.'

'A different sort of man,' she corrected him harshly. 'If it hadn't been for him, I couldn't have kept Davey.' Abruptly, her rage died and she became morose. 'On my own, I would never have been allowed to adopt him. I couldn't guarantee him a proper home, and with him to care for, I couldn't have taken a regular job or earned enough to keep us both.'

'But why tell you it was me?'

'Because I knew your reputation, I suppose.' Her eyes glittered fiercely. 'Get out the chastity belts, lock up your women-folk, here comes the Don Juan of Dyffryn! And since I knew,' she added caustically, 'I'd easily believe . . .'

'I wasn't as bad as that!' Gideon managed to look hurt. 'Maybe three or four over the years.'

'You were worse!' Ellis said it with relish. 'Besides, you always made a pet of Gwenny.'

'I told you,' he ground out between his teeth. 'It was less trouble that way. If I left her out of anything, she sulked and took it out on all of us. But that doesn't solve Davey's parentage; we'll have to look for somebody else.'

'Why?' she asked peremptorily. 'Isn't it obvious that Gwenny doesn't want whoever it was named? She lied to me to cover for him, and now she won't tell you. Perhaps she truly loved him. Maybe he was already married, maybe there's a wife somewhere, even children who could be hurt. And I have to think of Davey; he can't remember Robert but he has a photograph, and legally he's Robert's son.'

'I give up!' Gideon shook his head hopelessly. 'You're a pest, Ellis, you keep hammering away and you've got an answer for everything! Tell me, when we marry, will you expect me to adopt Davey?'

'No,' she frowned fiercely, reverting to practicality. 'He's my responsibility and I remember very well how you . . .' She hesitated fractionally before she revealed her hurt. 'You didn't want us here and you came all the way to London to tell me! You don't have much of an opinion of me, remember!'

'I didn't have, but then I was prejudiced against you from the start,' he explained gravely. 'You put Gwenny's nose out of joint, and I had to bear the brunt. I got the lot; how sly and secretive you were, how you played the good little girl to get round *Taid*, how Vanno always took your side in a squabble.' His hand across her mouth silenced her involuntary squeal of indignation as he continued reasonably. 'Your apparent desire for money and later, a wealthy, older man you'd obviously trapped into marriage; that was what it looked like at the time.'

Of course it had looked like that, one misconception giving weight to another. Ellis blinked nervously. And when he had come to see her in London, hadn't she done her best to foster the illusion? She had been too clever by half and damned herself in the process.

'But from the time I visited you in London,' Gideon had that wry twist of self-mockery about his mouth again, 'I began seeing you in a different light. Alongside Gwenny, you'd always seemed colourless, and, as she'd said, a sly, silent, secretive little thing! That evening, I learned a lot. You're neither sly nor silent, and within a few days of your return here I didn't care if you were the Scarlet Woman herself.' Gideon continued in so conversational a tone that, for a second or two, the words were just noises with no meaning. 'I love you, Ellis'—what he was saying began to make sense— 'and I don't give a damn about anything you've ever done or how much money you have or how you got it! I only want you! I understand . . .'

'Oh, you understand, do you?' The bit about loving and wanting got through. She needed so badly to believe it but she dared not; it would weaken her, and she waved a small fist under his nose. 'I don't give that for your understanding and I won't be forgiven, not by you! Compared with you, I'm a spotless angel.'

'You're a damn fool.' He was laughing as he captured her fist and held it firmly—it was still waving dangerously close to his eye. 'Will you be quiet and listen? You've done a good job on Davey, and if you haven't told Vanno the truth, you've done the next best thing; you've brought the boy home.'

'I wanted him to be where he belongs.' She heard herself sounding weak and went on defiantly. 'Where else should he be but among his own? Vanno's accepted him, she thinks he's ours and she's quite happy with that. I don't want you spoiling everything.'

'And you weren't even going to tell me?'

Ellis shrugged. 'Yes, I was, eventually. I was so sure I'd enjoy doing it.' Her voice died away and she squeaked with alarm as his arm came round her, holding her still and a long, firm finger held her chin so that she couldn't turn her face away. 'But I didn't want to see your face if you denied being his father,' she added.

'I didn't deny it when Vanno accused me.' There was a watchful expression in his dark eyes.

'No, you didn't.' Ellis huddled into herself miserably. 'You lied, but I suppose you were telling her what she wanted to hear.' All her protective instincts came to the fore and she almost grovelled. 'Please don't tell her about Gwenny, she's so proud of her.'

'Stop it!' He broke in sharply and when she didn't seem to hear him, he slapped her gently. When that had no effect, he shook her until she was dizzy and his voice was repeating those incredible things about loving and wanting so that she could hardly believe her ears. The same thing twice! Perhaps he really did mean it. She forgave him the slap and the shaking.

'My goodness! You don't give in easily, do you, woman? I tell you I love you, I want you and I'm going to have you and you aren't even listening!' He was muttering frustratedly. 'One hell of a married life we're going to have if you won't be quiet and let me love you. I want to kiss you and you keep gabbling.'

'I'm allowed to say what I think.' She said it automatically and bit her lip hard. She was spoiling everything. This was what she had wanted to hear ever since she had been sixteen, and now, when she was hearing it at last, she couldn't believe it. She said so.

'I don't believe it! You're up to something nasty, I know your sneaky ways!'

'All I'm up to is trying to make a little restrained

love to my future wife,' he riposted angrily. 'But if you don't want me to . . .'

Ellis had reached her limit, she thought she now knew a little of how Gwenny must have felt when faced with the choice of Davey or a career in the States. Or as Gwenny was feeling now, when the choice was between fame and a slide into mediocrity. There were no guarantees, but you had to go all out for what you wanted.

'Oh, but I do, I want it more than anything!' Her small hands clutched at him as if he might vanish at any moment, and her eyes were agonised. 'I'm starving for you, only I keep remembering. You turned me down once and you weren't kind about it. I mean, you could have been nicer, let me down gently instead of storming at me as if I had been the Whore of Babylon.' She shivered at the memory.

'Have some sense.' Gideon rasped it out through stiff lips as he slid out of his sheepskin jacket and hung it about her shoulders. She snuggled gratefully into the warmth of it; it smelled of pipe tobacco and Gideon, very heady, and much nicer than Chanel No 5. 'You were a child, barely out of school and as transparent as glass,' he scolded. 'Vanno had seen it coming on and I'd had my orders! Besides, very young virgins aren't my style.'

Ellis scowled. Gideon was behaving with an unusual restraint. Here she was; willing, eager even, and Gideon was *talking*! And after she had waited so long!

'I'm twenty-six, hardly very young, and I'm a widow, not a virgin,' she pointed out acidly, only to add belligerently, 'so what's stopping you now!'

His dark head swooped down, halting only when their faces were barely an inch apart. 'My little love,' he growled, 'I want better for you than the "*hen*" and a pile of straw.'

'It was good enough for your Nest,' she muttered defiantly, 'and she was used to the best. Or don't you believe the old story?'

'It could be true. You're sure?' He said it quietly before he removed a sleepy pup from its haven by her knees; closing the gap between them, and somehow it seemed quite right that he should.

Ellis clung to him closely. This was what she had dreamed of, and it was better than any dream. You didn't have to wait to die before you went to heaven. His black hair, which looked harsh, wasn't harsh at all. It was like strong silk clinging to her fingers, and she felt a tremor run through him as she touched the smooth skin on the back of his neck. Through the soft tweed of her skirt, she could feel him wanting her, and the straw and dim, drab surroundings paled into insignificance as her response grew. She even forgot Davey!

Straw, a feather-bed or even an interior-sprung mattress, what did it matter? She trembled as she felt his fingers stripping away the obstacles between them, she didn't feel cold when the air touched her shoulders. There was his weight on her, the feel of him, the smell of him and his voice murmuring in Welsh.

She couldn't understand a word but it sounded beautiful. Everything was beautiful and the '*hen*' suddenly seemed full of light. A light too bright for her eyes, and her eyelids closed, but still the brightness was there, all around her and pulsing in an age-old rhythm until it finally exploded in a shatter of fragments and she heard her own cry mingling with Gideon's hoarse murmurings.

It could have lasted minutes or hours. Ellis neither knew nor cared, and even the crackling straw and the bare stone walls couldn't spoil her comfort. She had a feeling of fulfilment, of coming home at last, of being perfectly content.

'I think I always knew it would end like this,' Gideon murmured against her breast. 'I told myself I despised you, yet when I came to London I drowned in your eyes. I fought it, *cariad*, I think I've been fighting it ever since you grew up, but you were always there at the back of my mind. And now, the fighting's over.'

He raised his head and brought her out of her dream world as he carefully tidied her up, and his smile was neither wry nor fiendish, only very tender. 'You look smug, my lovely; like a little cat that's got the cream.'

'So do you.' She blinked away tears as she wrinkled her nose at him, loving him with her eyes. 'But the time we've wasted! You should have done it my way.' A reminiscent smile curved her lips. 'It would have been hay, still warm from the sun and soft . . .'

His lips twitched; there was a teasing glint in his eyes and he shook his head at her reproachfully. 'Remind me in August or September; I must cure you of your fixation with hay. But I'll do better for you soon,' he promised. 'Our own home, our own room, our own bed, a lock on the door, all the nights and no hurry.'

'Don't say any more.' She looked up into his face with eyes which wouldn't focus properly because of her tears. 'I still can't really believe . . .'

'Believe, *cariad*! I'll make a habit of reminding you frequently.' Big hands cupped her face and dark eyes inspected her gravely. 'But now there's the matter of Gwenny.'

She blinked up at him. 'What about Gwenny?' Then, as reality came swooping back on her like a hawk and digging its talons in her flesh, 'Davey!' and she struggled to rise with only the weight of his hand on her breast preventing her. 'Please,' she implored huskily, 'you don't know . . .'

'But I do, sweetheart,' he countered annoyingly while his hand still kept her flat in the straw. 'You mean her threat to steal Davey; I'm just surprised at your believing it! Can you imagine Gwenny and the boy going off together? I can't! He'd have fought every inch of the way rather than be parted from his Ellis, and she'd have been bringing him back after fifteen minutes! As for that cheque you've given her, I think five thousand is a bit generous, but it's your money, you can give her the lot if you want to.'

'Oh, I couldn't do that, I've never thought of it as mine,' she explained gruffly. 'It's invested and most of the interest goes to charities. I can have anything I ask for, but I've only ever taken an allowance and I can stop that, if you'd rather. But if I do,' she added sturdily, 'I shall expect you to feed and clothe me. You might even have to help pay for the repairs to the lodge, but I'm quite a good cook and a very economical housekeeper.'

'That's my sort of woman; sexy, hardworking and economical.' Gideon silenced her temporarily with his mouth on hers and she sank mindlessly into his embrace. She could have wept when it ended and reality crept back in.

'What about later, when we have to tell Davey?' she asked hesitantly. 'I wouldn't like him to think badly of Gwenny.'

'Better you leave that to me.' Gideon gave her narrow shoulders a comforting squeeze. 'No sentimentality or dramatics. All man-to-man stuff.'

He broke off as the old door of the 'hen' groaned open. Ellis scrambled to her feet and peeping over the straw barrier, she watched as a filthy little boy slithered through the gap.

'You went to sleep, Ellis,' Davey accused her, 'so we took my puppy for a little walk and he fell in some mud. 'I'm a little bit dirty too but you did say I could be. I fink I'd better have a bath so can we have tea at Aunty Vanno's. We're awful hungry and Idris has made his new boots dirty.'

'Time to go.' Gideon said it with a regretful look as he brushed away the bits of straw clinging to Ellis's hair, gave her bottom a fond pat and dropped a kiss on the end of her nose. 'Back to Vanno's, my love; and on our best behaviour. She'll have a visitor!'

Davey's eyes were bright with suspicion as he sidled towards them. 'Why are you kissing my Ellis, Gideon?' he demanded.

'Because I'm going to marry her.' Gideon said it calmly, and Ellis watched as Davey stumped the last few steps. Would he accept . . .?

'Oh good!' Davey appraised the new situation and

had only one question to ask. 'Will you be my daddy or my uncle?'

'Which would you like better?' Gideon gave Ellis a warning tap and waited for the reply.

'We-ell,' Davey gave the matter more thought. 'I fink I'd rather you were my daddy.'

'That's good.' Gideon stepped around the bales of straw to take Davey's filthy little hand in his own big one. 'And we've a surprise for you.' He looked over his shoulder to give Ellis a smile and she drowned in the warm reassurance in it. 'Ellis, *annwylyd*, it's time we took Davey to meet his Aunty Gwenny!'

Davey's shrill pipe was filled with excitement. 'Did you hear that, Ellis? I've got you, a daddy, and *two* aunties! I fink I'll call Aunty Vanno "Grandma" so's I'll have one of everyfing!'

'And if you wait a bit longer,' Gideon pulled Ellis close and his arm was hard, warm and very reassuring while his eyes held a wicked promise as he continued gravely, 'Ellis and I will get you some little brothers and sisters.'

'Ooooh!' Davey's dark eyes were huge with a shining wonder and in the silence which followed, only Ellis heard Gideon's soft comment.

'Father unknown, but I'm grateful to him, whoever he was. Somehow, I can't imagine life without Davey!'

Davey plus a muddy pup skittered out of the *'hen'* and Ellis followed them with Gideon bringing up the rear. As the old door closed behind them, she drew in a deep breath and gazed about her. Was it her imagination, or had spring come to the valley?

With Gideon's possessive arm about her waist, she

paused and let her eyes wander over the steep slopes on the other side of the valley where sheep were wandering stolidly upwards, followed by their lambs. The sky was a pale blue over her head and the wind was funnelling up from the sea and stirring the tops of the trees.

'Worried about meeting Gwenny?' Gideon misunderstood her hesitation. 'Don't be, Ellis. You know her, she boils over like a kettle, says unforgivable things but she's always sorry afterwards.'

'I know that!' She raised her head and gave him a reassuring look. 'No, I only wanted to look at the scenery. When I was in London, I used to be so homesick for all this.'

'I couldn't bear to leave it for long either, but can you stand looking at it every day for the rest of your life?' He raised an eyebrow. 'You won't get bored with it, or your hick of a husband? A well-behaved husband,' he added, and his arm tightened about her. 'I've got my woman, my roving days are over.'

'How dull that makes you sound,' she teased and smiled delightedly as he gave her a lustful, leering look.

'Soon we'll be married and . . .' his leer intensified . . . 'I'm a man of many parts. The last thing you'll find me is *dull*!'

HARLEQUIN
Romance

Coming Next Month

Available in April wherever paperback books are sold, or through
Harlequin Reader Service:

In the U.S.
901 Fuhrmann Blvd.
P.O. Box 1397
Buffalo, N.Y. 14240-1397

In Canada
P.O. Box 603
Fort Erie, Ontario
L2A 5X3

You'll flip . . . your pages won't!
Read paperbacks *hands-free* with

Book Mate • I

The perfect "mate" for all your romance paperbacks

**Traveling • Vacationing • At Work • In Bed • Studying
• Cooking • Eating**

Perfect size for all standard paperbacks, this wonderful invention makes reading a pure pleasure! Ingenious design holds paperback books OPEN and FLAT so even wind can't ruffle pages – leaves your hands free to do other things. Reinforced, wipe-clean vinyl-covered holder flexes to let you turn pages without undoing the strap . . . supports paperbacks so well, they have the strength of hardcovers!

Pages turn WITHOUT opening the strap

SEE-THROUGH STRAP

Reinforced back stays flat

Built in bookmark

BOOK MARK

BACK COVER
HOLDING STRIP

10 x 7¼ opened.
Snaps closed for easy carrying, too

Available now. Send your name, address, and zip code, along with a check or money order for just $5.95 + .75¢ for postage & handling (for a total of $6.70) payable to Reader Service to:

Reader Service
Bookmate Offer
901 Fuhrmann Blvd.
P.O. Box 1396
Buffalo, N.Y. 14269-1396

Offer not available in Canada
*New York and Iowa residents add appropriate sales tax

BM-G

This April, don't miss Harlequin's new Award of
Excellence title from

elusive as the unicorn

*When Eve Eden discovered that Adam
Gardener, successful art entrepreneur, was
searching for the legendary English artist, The
Unicorn, she nervously shied away. The Unicorn's
true identity hit too close to home....*

*Besides, Eve was rattled by Adam's
mesmerizing presence, especially in the light
of the ridiculous coincidence of their names—
and his determination to take advantage of it!
But Eve was already engaged to marry her
longtime friend, Paul.*

*Yet Eve found herself troubled by the different
choices Adam and Paul presented. If only the
answer to her dilemma didn't keep eluding her....*

HPI258-I